# Missing With

## A Sanford 3rd Age Club Mystery

## David W Robinson

in association with Ocelot Press

*Ocelot Press*

© David W Robinson 2025
All right reserved

Edited by Maureen Vincent-Northam

No part of this book may be used or reproduced in any manner whatsoever without written permission of the author except for brief quotations used for promotion or in reviews. This is a work of fiction. Names, characters, and incidents are used fictitiously.

# Chapter One

Brenda Jump's eyes flickered open, and she closed them again right away when a pounding headache hit home. It begged the question: what kind of cocktails was she drinking last night and how much of it had she taken in?

A thought struck her. In that brief second or two when her eyes were open, she did not recognise her surroundings. It didn't look like her comfortable, well-appointed bedroom, and she was certain that it was not Joe Murray's place, the only other bed she shared, albeit on infrequent occasions. True, Joe's place was a bit of a dump (he was a man living alone, what else would she expect?) but it wasn't quite as dark and barren as her present surroundings appeared.

Apart from anything else, she had a distinct memory of a sumptuous meal and saying goodnight to Stewart Dalmer (not Joe, not Sheila, certainly not George Robson) when their taxi dropped her off outside her home, but she couldn't recall actually letting herself in. Perhaps, she suggested to herself, the memories were false, generated by whatever wondrous cocktails she had been drinking.

Slowly, cautiously, she opened her eyes again, and the first inkling of worry entered her head.

The light was stark and singular. A single, shaded bulb above her head, shining straight down upon her and casting a dull illumination around the barren room. The minimal light was enough, however, to let her take in the dour surroundings of bare, windowless, concrete walls and a stout steel door. The place had an odour of fustiness, decay, as if it had not been used in a long while. Definitely not Joe's place, nor George Robson's.

This could not be real. This was some kind of nightmare, and any moment now she would wake to find Joe snuggling up to her. Never the most romantic of men, Joe nevertheless paid rigorous attention to post-coital snuggling.

She made to get up and found she could not, and for the first time, she realised she was not lying down but sitting on an uncomfortable chair. She tugged at her arms. They were bound to the back of the wooden seat. An attempt to move her legs proved equally fruitless. They were bound to the chair, too.

That settled it. She was definitely dreaming. Better to relax and wait until she woke up naturally. Doubtless someone – Sheila was the expert on dreams and their meaning – would come up with some ghastly, Freudian interpretation, probably based on her absolute refusal to end her widowhood and remarry. Colin had been the only man in her life and if she chose to enjoy herself occasionally with other partners, it did not mean she intended settling down with anyone. Even if she thought about it, the only candidate would be Joe, but he was not in the frame. Divorced and enjoying life in his mid to late fifties, he felt the same as her. If God had meant couples to be manacled together, he would have fitted them with inbuilt handcuffs.

Why, though, would she dream of a dark,

dismal cell like this?

She wasn't really into the kind of esoteric reading Sheila sometimes enjoyed, so dream symbols were slightly out of her league. Still, she tried.

Was the cell an indication that she felt trapped by life? And bound hand and foot to the chair? Another indication that she was tied to her life, and the fact that it was a rickety dining room chair rather than a comfortable settee might indicate that she may have found her life comfortable once upon a time, but it was old, out of date, stale. That idea could be further supported by the fustiness of the cell. It was time to break out, seek fresh pastures.

She focussed on the word 'cell'. It was perhaps the wrong word. Her knowledge of prison accommodation was gleaned from television, and she imagined cells to be small, cramped little places with two beds and minimal facilities. This was larger and had absolutely no facilities. A low, arched ceiling, no washbasin, no toilet, no bunk. There were several large posters pinned to the walls around her. One in particular took her eye, but she still felt groggy and could not make much of it out in the poor lighting. It seemed to be some kind of alphabetic list, but of what, she did not know.

Matters to either side were no improvement. There were what appeared to be work benches, but she could see no tools, no fixtures, no equipment of any description. It was more like a bunker, which only signalled that, as dreams went, this was beyond bizarre.

She heard the rattle of a key or a bolt on the

outside of the door and prepared herself for whatever nightmare might walk in. Joe with a garish red face and demonic horns? George Robson, another of her infrequent bedmates, made up like an evil clown, or perhaps Stewart Dalmer, a man who had made the odd effort to secure her favours, including a sumptuous meal last night, dressed in a formal business suit, but carrying the lever which would operate the gallows or guillotine?

The door creaked open on badly lubricated hinges, and he stepped in. A black balaclava covering his head and some kind of black clothing from head to foot, and the only part of him clearly visible was his right hand carrying what looked like a tripod. As he stepped in, so his left hand became visible and in it he carried a large bucket.

'Ah, Mrs Jump. You're awake. Sorry about the head, but I had to subdue you. Half-drunk you might have been, but you were not very co-operative.' His voice was distorted, as if it came through some kind of synthesiser, but did she detect a fairly strong Yorkshire bias? Or was that her worried mind roaming again? He nodded to the bucket. 'This is your toilet, and once you're done with it, you're going to become a video star.'

He crossed the rough floor to her, put the tripod and bucket down and in the poor light, she could see a camcorder attached to the tripod.

How much stranger would this dream become?

Then he began to manhandle her, tugging the ropes on her wrists and feet and when he had freed her, he yanked her to her feet. Her legs were weak and she almost collapsed, but he maintained a

strong grip on her arm and pointed at the bucket.
And the full horror of her situation hit Brenda. This was a nightmare, all right, but it was no dream.

# Chapter Two

No matter what the time of year, even in the mad dash around Christmas, Joe Murray, Sheila Riley and Brenda Jump would take their break at any time between half past nine and half past on every morning of the week. In the early months of the New Year, the timing was not an issue, and they could comfortably leave the running of The Lazy Luncheonette to the other staff, Lee, his wife Cheryl, and their friend and general assistant Kayleigh Watson. It was a flexible routine, one which had been in place since Joe took over the running of the place from his father, and the two women, Sheila and Brenda came on board.

Only not now. Wednesday February 19, a good seven weeks into the year, and Brenda was noticeable by her absence for the second day in succession. Even the draymen whose great joy was exchanging mild insults with Joe, had commented on it.

'Valentine's last Friday, Joe, so did you wear her out?' asked Barry Standish, one of Joe's greatest goaders. 'Or have you got her chained up in your cellar, keeping her as a kitchen slave?'

As always, Joe gave as good as he got, but no one could explain Brenda's absence.

'Two days,' Joe complained as Sheila joined him at table five for their regular morning break, 'and not a word from her.'

Sat opposite, Sheila was just as concerned. 'It's

so unlike her, Joe.'

'You're sure she's not at home?'

Sheila tutted. 'Joe, we all three have keys for each other's houses, don't we? When I couldn't get an answer yesterday, I thought the same as you. She's at home and had an accident. I had visions of her laid on the floor unconscious, so I let myself in. She's not there. And when I checked, there's none of her clothing missing, so it's not as if she's gone away on holiday or anything.'

'She wouldn't do that anyway. Not so early in the year, and not without letting us know in advance.'

'Have you checked with Gemma?'

Joe shook his head. 'I don't wanna call the police for what might be something and nothing. Do we know where she was on Monday night?'

'As far as I know she went out for a meal with Stewart Dalmer. He actually invited her for Valentine's, but she cried off.' Sheila cast a demeaning glance at Joe. 'She already had a Valentine's date with you, didn't she? Anyway, it was Stewart's birthday or something. And before you ask, yes I checked with him and he says they shared a taxi which dropped her off at home about eleven o'clock Monday night. That, Joe, is the last anyone saw or heard anything of her.' Sheila paused to drink from her beaker, lending urgency to her next announcement. 'I think we should call the police.'

Joe hedged. His niece, Detective Inspector Gemma Craddock, was nominal head of Sanford CID, and the station commander, Chief

Superintendent Terry Cummins, was a friend of many years standing, but he doubted they would take kindly to him calling them for a missing woman when it wasn't absolutely certain that Brenda was missing. Aside from anything else, like any other police force in the country, they were rushed off their feet. When weren't they?

A major part of the problem was Brenda herself. Like Sheila, she was widowed, but unlike her best friend, she dated a number of men, Joe included, and her determination to enjoy life had garnered an unjustified reputation for sleeping around. Both Joe and Sheila knew that it bore no resemblance to reality, but that did nothing to deter the gossip mongers of Sanford. In the eyes of the great unwashed, she was little better than a loose-legged merry widow, a pushover. As long as she did not hear it, Brenda did not give a fig for what people thought or said about her, but in the present circumstances, that would only fuel speculation that she had shot off somewhere abroad with some man friend and simply not bothered to tell anyone, including her best friends at The Lazy Luncheonette. Her reputation was also well known to the police, and Joe could imagine the response he would get from Gemma and Cummins.

'Maybe we should ring round the hospitals first,' he suggested.

'I already phoned Sanford General and they wouldn't talk to me. Patient confidentiality, they said, but I have a friend in admin, and she privately admitted that Brenda had not been seen there. And I can't see how she could end up in Leeds or

Wakefield without going through Sanford first. No, Joe, Stewart is adamant that she was fine when he dropped her off on Monday night.' She checked her watch. 'Thirty-six hours now, and no one has seen or heard from her. We should speak to either Terry Cummins or Gemma.'

Joe capitulated and rang his niece, only to get her voicemail. He cut the call without leaving a message and rang Terry Cummins, only to be told that the Chief Superintendent was at a meeting in Leeds.

'Why don't we leave it until the Miners Arms tonight?' he suggested. 'I can make an announcement at the disco, see if anyone can tell us anything.'

With a reluctant nod, Sheila agreed. 'But I don't know what they might know that I don't… Oh. Wait. What about her sister-in-law? Dorothy.'

'The Oxford snob? What? You think Brenda may have shot off down there without telling us? It's not very likely. For a start off, she didn't like Dorothy, and even if there was some emergency down there, I'm sure Brenda would have phoned one of us.'

'You're probably right, but I'll ring Dorothy anyway.' Sheila took out her phone.

'Remind her of that time I got her off the hook in Blackpool during Twixmas.'

But as Joe suggested, it was a non-starter. Dorothy Kinley, Brenda's late husband's divorced sister, had neither seen nor heard from Brenda for months.

'That's it,' Joe declared. 'Unless the members

can tell us anything tonight, I'm out of ideas.'

The situation was not improved an hour later when Gemma Craddock turned up.

'Here's another cop looking for a handout,' Joe quipped as he poured a beaker of tea for her. 'Want a bite to eat?'

'A sandwich would go down well, Uncle Joe, but I'm here on business, not socialising.'

Calling for Cheryl to relieve him on the counter and leave the kitchen to her husband, Lee, and their assistant, Kayleigh, Joe supplied tea and a tuna salad sandwich for his niece, and joined her and Sheila at table five.

'I'm glad you've called,' he said, 'but let's hear what you want first.'

Gemma dipped into her briefcase and came out with a wanted poster. 'Con on the run, and we'd like you to pin this up in your window, if you will. As it happens he's one of your old cases. Vic Atherton. Remember him?' She handed Joe the poster and he studied it.

*Police are seeking the whereabouts of Victor Atherton, serving a four-year sentence for car theft. He was granted home leave to attend the funeral of a close family member, but failed to return to prison.*

*A native of Sanford, Atherton is described as 54 years of age, white, and 5'11" tall, slender, with dark, thinning hair. He is known to be short-tempered and can turn violent if provoked. Members of the public seeing him are advised to keep their distance and contact their nearest police station or call Crimestoppers.*

Joe raked his memory. 'Not sure I've ever heard of him. You're sure he's one of mine?'

Gemma bit into the sandwich. 'Yorkshire Jewellers a few years back. You caught him and his girlfriend at the time, pulling some scam with an expensive ring.'

Bells rang in Joe's head. 'Oh, yeah. I remember him. What was his girlfriend's name?' He raked his memory again. 'Fiona. Fiona... Watson.' He leaned back on his chair and called over his shoulder. 'Kayleigh, come here a minute, luv.'

Kayleigh, the newest recruit to The Lazy Luncheonette's crew, approached with an air of timidity. 'Have I done something wrong, Uncle Joe?' She always addressed him as "Uncle Joe" even though she was not a relative.

'No more than usual,' Joe told her. 'It's not you, chicken, but your family. We know Pauline, your sister, but do you have another sister or an aunt called Fiona?'

Kayleigh nodded vigorously. 'Oh, yeah. Auntie Fi. We don't talk about her. She's me dad's sister, and she went to prison for thieving from the shop where she worked. Her and her fella. Uncle Vic. Course, he was married at the time and carrying on with her. None of us liked him. Anyway, she's dead is Aunty Fi. Mam told me she passed on about a year ago.'

'A year is about right, Kayleigh,' Gemma said. 'Ovarian cancer diagnosed too late. Atherton was inside at the time – again – and granted home leave twice: first to marry her just before she died, and then for her funeral. Anyway, his mother passed away two or three weeks back. He got home leave again for the funeral, but this time, he never went back to the nick. There's a general call out for him and it's focussed here, in Sanford. Well, he is Sanford born and bred.'

Joe smiled at Kayleigh, indicating that she should get back to the kitchen to help Lee prepare lunches.

Sheila commented for the first time since Gemma's arrival. 'You said he was in prison again. Was this not for the theft Joe caught him on?'

'Hell, no. He got eight months for that, and Fiona got three months for aiding and abetting. With that kind of conviction behind him – and her – they couldn't get work anywhere. Certainly not in a jeweller's shop. They were living on Leeds Road Estate, not far from where you used to live, Joe, and getting by on benefits. She was done twice more for shoplifting, and he was taking such work as he could find, usually cleaning or labouring or stuff like that. Always cash in hand. His time inside toughened him up, made him a temperamental sod and he got into fights regular. Then he nicked a car, didn't he? Got four years for it. He's about a year or more into that and as I say, he went AWOL after his mother's funeral last month.' Gemma shook her head. 'It'll cost him all of his remission. When – if – we get him back, he'll serve the full four years plus whatever the beaks decide to add on for absconding.'

'So how did he get away from his prison escort?'

'He didn't have an escort, Joe,' Gemma

replied. 'He's in – correction – was in an open prison and given three days leave, and ordered to report to us every day. He did for the first two days, then disappeared. It's a trust system. They fully expected him to come back.'

'Blown his trust then, hasn't he?' Joe said. 'I do remember him now. Like Kayleigh said, he had an ex-wife kicking around somewhere, and he said the divorce was costing him an arm and a leg, which was why he nicked that expensive shiner from the shop.'

'Already checked the ex out, Joe,' Gemma told them. 'The only thing she's willing to give him is a round of applause when he's frogmarched back to the nick, and even then, she'll be cheering for us plod. She worships the very ground he's got coming to him. But we have eyes on her just in case she's flannelling.' Gemma finished the last bite of her sandwich and washed it down with a mouthful of tea. 'So what's with you two?'

Joe frowned. 'Come again? Us two?'

'You said you were glad I'd called. Something in the wind... and where's Brenda? Sick or holiday?'

Joe and Sheila exchanged a glance, and Joe invited, 'You tell her.'

Over the next few minutes Sheila outlined the mystery of Brenda's absence and the steps both she and Joe had taken to find their friend. Gemma listened and when Sheila was finished, she took a moment to consider the situation.

'I'm not knocking her, but we all know what Brenda's like when it comes to men. It's all right you two saying you know all her men friends, but do you? And you can't categorically say that she went missing after Stewart Dalmer dropped her off on Monday night. For all you know, she could have got a phone call from another man, and decided to shoot off with him first thing yesterday morning.'

'All her clothing's still in the wardrobe,' Sheila protested.

'Can you absolutely guarantee that? Come on, Sheila, you don't live with her, and for all you know, she could be travelling light. Hell, it could be someone who's proposed to her and she decided to do a runner to Bethnal Green—'

'You mean Gretna Green,' Joe interrupted.

'Wherever. You know what I mean. I'll put feelers out, see if anyone's turned anything up, but right now, I've more on my plate than looking for someone like Brenda. The economy's its usual mess, leaving a lot of people strapped for cash, and we've all on to cope with the usual shoplifters and burglars and drunken brawls after the pubs shut. Unless you come across anything to suggest that she's come to harm, we don't really have the resources to put into it.'

Joe held Sheila's stare. 'Told you.'

Sheila ignored him and carried on speaking to Gemma. 'It's the weekly, 3rd Age Club disco at the Miners Arms tonight, and Joe and I have already agreed to see if the members know anything. Beyond that, if there's nothing else you can do, Gemma, we'll keep you informed of anything we turn up.'

'Cool,' Gemma agreed. 'And it's time for me

to love you and leave you. Just keep your eyes open for Atherton, Joe. He blames you for all of his problems, and his time in the nick has turned him into a nasty piece of work.'

Joe snorted. 'If he turns up here, he'll learn about nasty.'

Gemma laughed and gathered together her belongings. 'Joe, you couldn't fight your way past a gang of toddlers in Mothercare. Thanks for the sandwich. Don't forget to pin that poster up for us, and I'll catch you both later.'

Joe moved to the counter, collected a roll of adhesive tape and followed his niece to the exit, where he affixed the wanted poster to the inside of the large windows.

'Just what we need, innit?' he said to Sheila as he took his place behind the counter. 'Brenda missing and a lag I helped send down on the run.'

# Chapter Three

At least, Brenda thought, he hadn't blindfolded her.

Not that being able to see did her much good. Even with the small light he left her, there was nothing to see in the barren cell (she could think of no other word to describe it) other than the posters on the wall, most of which seemed to concentrate on procedure in the event of a nuclear attack or major breakdown in communication.

The one thing she could say was that the place was old. Wherever she was, it had not been used for several years, and those various information boards led her to the conclusion that it was something to do with the military. Thinking it over, she decided it was a nuclear bunker and that led her to a second conclusion. She was nowhere near Sanford. Aside from a small, now defunct base which was used by the Territorial Army once upon a time, Sanford had never entertained the army or the air force, and forty or fifty miles from the sea, the navy was not an option.

It would be so much easier, she thought, if she could move around, but this evil man (despite his efforts to disguise his voice, she was one hundred percent certain that her abductor was male) kept her bound to the chair at all times. Even when he videoed her, she remained tied to the chair and he only released her to let her eat, drink and use the bucket. To her fury and embarrassment, he did not even have the decency to turn his back, but kept his eye on her while she relieved herself.

It was bitter cold in the cell, and that was aggravated by loathing and not a little fear. When he returned earlier, she was convinced that he was going to murder her, but then he sat her in front of the video camera and holding up a tablet, compelled her to read out his message. That told her his intentions were different. Not that it meant he would not kill her; merely that he would not kill her for the time being, and she consoled herself with the thought that while she was alive, there was always the chance that someone would find her.

So she hoped.

Everything about him frightened her. Brenda Jump was no coward, but this man's cold determination, complete emotional detachment, induced feelings of absolute dread.

It would not be the only video he would send. Although he hadn't said so, the one he forced her to record, the one aimed at her friends, gave Sheila and Joe no specific instructions, and if he was to secure a ransom (why else would he be holding her?) he would need to do so. That, in turn, meant he would compel her to record at least one more video. She had time. Time to think, time to work out some means of signalling to her friends and, if she knew anything about them they would go to the police.

She looked around the derelict room again. How could she do it? What kind of system could she use to let them know she was being held in a military bunker?

Fear, spiked her thought processes, and then she saw the means. She would have to learn the different codes for each letter of the alphabet. A daunting task, especially in the poor illumination afforded by the single lamp he left switched on, but she had nothing else to do with her time while she sat, bound to this uncomfortable chair.

# Chapter Four

Joe walked into his house at about eleven o'clock that evening and he was in one of the worst moods he could remember for a long time.

The 3rd Age Club's weekly disco was one of the highlights of the week, not only for him, but for many of the members, and yet, despite it being one of the last ones of the (technical) winter, a time when they usually began to look forward to their frequent spring, summer and autumn outings, Joe had managed to bring the mood down with an early announcement on Brenda's (assumed) disappearance.

No one could offer information or constructive suggestions, but when details of Brenda's activities on Monday night came out, many accusing eyes turned upon Stewart Dalmer.

Dalmer was a long-standing member but unlike most of the 3rd Age Club he was concerned less with enjoying himself, more with pursuing his business activities as a local antiques dealer. To Joe's certain knowledge, he had few friends in the club, but one of them was Brenda. He had challenged Joe several times for the chairmanship of the club, without success. Neither Joe nor Sheila imagined for one moment that Dalmer was involved with Brenda's disappearance, and they had to step in to prevent open warfare in the top room of the Miners Arms, a situation which gathered momentum when George Robson, a burly, foreman gardener in the employ of Sanford Borough Council and also one of Brenda's regular dates, challenged Dalmer.

'Knock it off, all of you,' Joe called from the small podium. 'Especially you, George. One of our friends, no less a person than our treasurer, is missing and we won't find her by falling out with one another.'

George pointed an accusing finger at Dalmer. 'If he's hurt her, I'll—'

'Oh, shut up, you fat idiot,' Dalmer interrupted.

George moved towards him, but Les Tanner and Alec Staines got in the way, and pressed him back.

'I said knock it off, George,' Joe ordered. 'Stop behaving like a total dick. Nobody's accusing Stewart of anything.'

Sheila took the microphone from him. 'We had a word with Gemma Craddock this morning, and the police have enough on their plate as it is. Don't they always? They don't have the manpower to start a search for Brenda, especially when we can't confirm that she's genuinely missing. All Joe and I can suggest is first, if you know anything, speak to us. In private if you prefer. Beyond that, we're asking that we all, each and every one of us, keep our eyes open and our ears to the ground for any hint of where she might be.'

'Have you checked with your missus in Tenerife, Joe?' Alec Staines asked. 'Maybe Brenda's gone there so they could compare notes on you.'

Joe had the feeling that Alec's comment was

intended to lighten the mood, but it didn't work. He confined himself to a scowl, Sheila berated Alec, while Julia, Alec's wife, kept her voice to a whisper when she scolded him.

When the general debate was over, Joe set up and ran the evening's music but few people were in the mood for dancing.

He made his way to the bar, ordered drinks for himself and Sheila, and collared Dalmer. 'I know I'm badgering you, Stewart, but was there anything unusual about Monday night?'

'Nothing,' Dalmer admitted. 'We had a cracking meal at Churchill's, a bit of dancing, I took her home, a goodnight kiss, and watched her until she was safely in the house. Then I went home. I did try to ring her yesterday, Tuesday morning and evening, but I didn't get an answer. Just to say thanks for Monday night.'

'You didn't try getting her at The Lazy Luncheonette though, did you?'

'I wouldn't do that, Joe. If I need to speak to someone on the phone, I tend not to disturb them during working hours. I assumed she would be at work, first thing, so I rang her about six in the morning, presuming it would be before she left for work, and then at five in the afternoon, and when she didn't answer, I thought no more about it. Come on, Joe, no one's kidding anyone. Brenda dates a number of men, you included, and for all I knew, she was out with another guy.' He scowled across the floor at George Robson. 'You shouldn't listen to that fat fool. Even if Brenda and I had fallen out, I wouldn't resort to violence of any description. I never do.'

'That's just George being George. He had Brenda to himself for long enough so take no notice. On the other hand, if you do hear anything of or from Brenda, give me a bell, will you? Even if it's during the day. I can always find two minutes to talk to people on the phone.'

From there, he exchanged a few frank, even harsh words with George Robson and one or two other people who had been too quick to jump on the "accuse Dalmer" bandwagon, and then got into a long debate with Les Tanner, concerning Brenda and her possible safety but which eventually degenerated into Tanner's customary criticism of Joe's administrative abilities or lack of same. The argument went on for the better part of forty-five minutes before Joe finally snapped and told Tanner to, 'Put a sock in it for crying out loud. We're more concerned for Brenda than your nitpicking.'

At that point Sheila and Sylvia Goodson, Tanner's partner, had to intervene to prevent war breaking out on a second front.

The evening showed no sign of improvement and at ten-thirty, he packed away the disco equipment, climbed into his car and drove home, only to trip over a bundle of mail on the doormat.

He cursed the postman, but in fact it had more to do with him than the postal service. Normally, he would call home after The Lazy Luncheonette closed, but he and Sheila stayed behind manning the phones until almost seven o'clock, ringing anyone and everyone they could think of, including Joe's ex-wife, Alison, who lived in Playa de Las

Américas, Tenerife, seeking any hint as to Brenda's whereabouts. That final call was the reason he was so short when Alec Staines mentioned Alison.

He picked the mail up and as he made his way to the kitchen, where he switched on the kettle for a final cup of tea before bed, and while he waited for it to come to the boil, he sorted through the envelopes: mostly junk mail, a reminder from the DVLA that the road fund on his car was due at the beginning of April, two credit card statements and a letter from the bank advising him of revised interest rates. He threw away the leaflets, filed the official mail and as the kettle boiled he was left with a single, small, padded envelope.

It was a puzzle. He could not recall ordering anything that might require such a small envelope, and a padded one to boot. Carrying his cup of tea to the living room, switching on the gas fire, he noticed that it had no postmark meaning it had been delivered by hand. He opened it and inside found a USB memory stick and a printed note instructing him to, "watch it".

He powered up his laptop and waited impatiently for it to go through its boot routine. He was no IT expert but he knew enough to run virus and malware scans on the memory stick and any files it contained before opening them.

There was only one file on it; an mp4 video file. After running more scans on it, satisfied that it was safe, he opened the file and his colour drained.

Apparently tied to a chair, light coming from above her, Brenda's face was illuminated by a powerful lamp which shone straight into her eyes.

Joe guessed she was cold, but that aside, she was shaking and afraid, and she did not look straight at the camera but slightly off to one side. Joe could not see her arms, so once again, he assumed she was tied to her chair, and the camera was zoomed in so close that he could make out little of the background.

When she spoke, her voice was shaky, croaky and she was near to tears. 'Sheila, Joe. I've been kidnapped. He was waiting in my house—'

'Stick to the script.' The harshened voice sounded as if it was run through a voice synthesiser and the owner was obviously behind the camera.

Brenda went on. 'You'll receive instructions. If you want to see me alive again, you have to...' She trailed off as a sob caught in her throat.

'Read it,' said the invisible voice.

'I'm sorry... I'm... I'm frightened.'

'Read. Now.'

Brenda focussed on the camera. 'If you want to see me again, my loves, you must follow the instructions. You. Not the police.'

And with that the screen blanked out.

Joe remained frozen to his seat, unable to move, unable to take his eyes off the blank screen, unable to think of anything other than the short, appalling action he had just witnessed.

He snapped himself out of it. His brain began to work again. Brenda had a wonderful sense of humour but this, he knew, was no joke. She had been kidnapped, and he had to decide on his next move.

Unable to clear his mind, he ran the video again

and this time listened more carefully, not to Brenda but the voice of the hidden kidnapper. It was not natural. He was sure that there were electronic bits and pieces you could buy which would alter the human voice, make it sound like some kind of robot. Despite the perilous thoughts scrambling his brain, a slow smile crossed his wrinkled features. Well, if there were such devices, then surely there were also police specialists who operated the kind of equipment which could unscramble such voices?

He gathered his wits, took out his smartphone and first rang Sheila to tell her the news. He was behind the times.

'I got a copy of it, too, Joe. I'm stunned. I can't take it in. I keep thinking it's all some gigantic joke.'

'Brenda has a smashing sense of humour but even she wouldn't go to these lengths.' Joe pulled himself together. 'Okay. First thing is not to panic. I think Brenda is in real danger, but running around like headless chickens won't do her or us any favours. I'll bell Gemma now, see what she has to say, and then I'll speak to Lee. We'll let him and Cheryl and Kayleigh open up in the morning. They can always bring a couple of casuals in to help with the rush. So don't go to work first thing. I'll ring back when I've spoken to Gemma and we'll probably have to go to Gale Street and the police station instead.'

'All right, Joe, but if anything happens to Brenda I'll never forgive you… or me. One of us should have been with her on Monday night.'

Joe disagreed. 'She was with Dalmer,

remember, and he insisted she got into the house fine, so don't beat yourself up, Sheila. There's no way we can babysit her twenty-four-seven. Let's try to be optimistic. We'll get her back in one piece.'

Killing the call, Joe wished his last words had sounded more positive.

He rang Gemma and she responded with typical irritation. 'Do you know what time it is, Joe? Some of us have proper jobs to go to tomorrow.'

'Yeah, yeah, I know, but it's urgent. Brenda's been kidnapped.'

'Oh, for God's sake, Joe—'

'No, please listen to me, Gemma, it's for real. I've received a video. So has Sheila.'

The urgency in his voice compelled her to listen, and over the next few minutes he told her of the video, Brenda's fear and the kidnapper's faked voice. By the time he was through, Gemma had ceased to be his niece and was once again the professional police officer.

'Right, Joe, I want you and Sheila at the station first thing tomorrow. Say, half past eight. I'll get a message to Terry Cummins asking him to be there early. Technically, he's at a conference in Leeds, but we'll need him at Gale Street because if anyone has to talk to Division, it's him. And Joe, don't go shoving your oar in. If this guy is serious – and it sounds like he is – he'll be lethal.'

'Lethal? I'll show him lethal if I get my hands on him.'

'Hot air, and you know it. You never were a scrapper. Just do as I ask, Joe.'

'No way will I sit back and do nothing.' Joe

heaved in a shaking breath. 'Anyway, I'll buzz off for now and see you first thing.'

Killing the call, he rang Sheila again and told her of Gemma's request and stressed that she should bring her copy of the video with her. From there he rang Lee and it was Cheryl who answered. 'What are you doing ringing at this time of night, Joe?'

'I'm sorry, lass, but it's an emergency. I need Lee to open up tomorrow morning. Sheila and I will be at Gale Street. Can you bell Kayleigh first thing, get her in early, and if you need more help, call on the usual casuals.'

'Sure, but what kind of an emergency is it?'

'I don't really want to say anything, Cheryl. Not until we're absolutely sure, but it's to do with Brenda.'

'Oh my God. Has she been taken ill or something? Cos it must be serious for you to ring at this hour.'

'More something than ill,' Joe admitted. 'I can't say too much, Cheryl, but Sheila and I will be at the cop shop first thing and I'll bring you all up to speed after we've seen Gemma and Terry Cummins. Now be a good girl, and open up with Lee in the morning.'

'Will do and don't forget to keep us posted.'

# Chapter Five

Joe was almost out on his feet when he arrived at Gale Street police station just before half past eight on Thursday morning, and Sheila did not look much livelier. Both had spent many years crawling out of bed early – any time between half past four and five o'clock in Joe's case – but under normal circumstances it would be on the back of at least six hours' sleep. According to his calculations, he had had no more than two or three hours and that was in fits and starts.

Sheila confessed to similar problems. 'I couldn't help thinking about her,' she said as they walked into the police station.

'Me neither.' Anger began to overtake him. 'If I could get my hands on him…' He trailed off half expecting the usual response to his lacking of fighting ability. It had been with him ever since his schooldays half a century back.

'Yes, Joe, I know how you feel but right now it's more important to get Brenda back healthy and in one piece.'

It came as no surprise when they were led straight upstairs to Cummins's office. The chief superintendent greeted them with a grim face.

At the start of his police career, Terry Cummins was a community constable in Sanford. His progress into CID, and his gradual promotion saw him move to York where he enjoyed something of a peripatetic role, working all over North Yorkshire.

He secured the Sanford station commander's post after the previous incumbent, Don Oughton retired.

Almost as soon as they made themselves comfortable, Gemma joined them and her features were just as dour as her chief's.

Joe handed over the memory stick, Gemma, wearing forensic gloves, inserted it into Cummins's computer, scanned it for viruses and malware, and happy that it was safe, ran the short film.

When it was through no one said anything for a few moments. It was as if the enormity of the message struggled to meet with their vision of life in Sanford.

It was Gemma who spoke first. 'Joe, Sheila, obviously you've both handled these memory sticks, so we'll need your prints for elimination.'

'No problem,' Joe agreed and Sheila nodded her confirmation.

Gemma faced her boss. 'I'll copy this, sir, and get the originals off to analysis in Leeds. I don't know what they'll be able to tell us but we're going to need every scrap of help we can muster.'

Joe spoke up. 'Well, surely you have people who can backward engineer the audio track. His voice, I'm talking about. Get it something like the original.'

'Assuming it is a voice and not computer generated, yes,' Cummins agreed, and promptly shifted the subject sideways. 'Brenda wasn't looking straight at the camera. She was reading the script, wasn't she?'

The question was aimed at Gemma but it was Joe who replied. 'That much is obvious, but she must have struggled to read it with the light shining straight into her face.'

'Tablet, Joe,' Sheila commented. 'Even dazzled, she would still be able to read the wording on a tablet.'

'The light is showing some of the background, but not enough,' Gemma said. 'I think our tech people should be able to bring up the background brightness. He focussed the camera so close on Brenda that I don't know it will tell us much but we might just get an idea of the kind of building she's being held in.'

'And what do we do in the meantime?' Joe demanded.

'The same as the rest of us, Joe,' Cummins said. 'Sit and worry. There's nothing else we can do.'

Joe would not hear it. 'No way. We go back half a century or more, me and Sheila and Brenda, and Brenda is in serious trouble. Hell, Terry, you've known her since you were a beat bobby here in Sanford. How long ago is that? Twenty, twenty-five years? There must be something we can do.'

The station commander shrugged. 'If you have ideas, I'm listening.' He turned to Gemma. 'While you're on the horn to tech services in Leeds, I'll speak to Ray Dockerty. We're likely to need support teams, possibly an armed unit, and definitely a negotiator. I don't think we need them here now, but we'll need them on standby.' Cummins swung his attention back to Joe. 'How many people know about this?'

'The video? Just Joe and me,' Sheila replied,

'but a lot of people know that Brenda is missing.'

'It was the big talking point at the Wednesday disco last night,' Joe told them. 'but like Sheila says we haven't told anyone about this message. Not even the kids at The Lazy Luncheonette.'

'Keep it to yourselves for now.' The superintendent tutted. 'Mind, with your mob of born again teenagers, it'll be difficult to keep it under wraps. Your crowd all have bigger mouths than the Humber. And I don't exclude your staff at The Lazy Luncheonette from that.'

While he recognised the accuracy of Cummins's word, Joe nevertheless bristled. 'We need people like them on our side, Terry. People who care about Brenda. Lee and Cheryl have grown up with her in the background, and the 3rd Age Club will fight tooth and nail to get her back in one piece. And don't forget, our members are spread all over Sanford, so who better to keep their eyes and ears open?'

'I'm not arguing about that, Joe, but you know what Chinese whispers are like. By the time the tale spreads, it'll be hacked into pieces… Yes, and so will Brenda, and fantasies like that could panic our man into actually doing it.'

'There is something else, sir,' Gemma put in. All eyes turned on her. 'I don't want to be any the more doom and gloom than we are already, but this message came by video. We don't know how much he made Brenda record.'

Joe was slow to latch on, but Sheila got there immediately. 'You mean he may have made her record all the messages, even those we haven't had yet, at one go, and then…' she trailed off obviously reluctant to put her thoughts into words.

Joe was appalled. 'He could have already snuffed her. Is that what you're trying to say?' No one answered and he took that as general assent. 'Oh, great. Cheer us up why don't you?'

'Take it easy, Joe,' Cummins advised. 'We're only trying to be practical. In this kind of situation, you should hope for the best, but anticipate the worst, so if it comes to it, you're prepared.' Again the superintendent focussed on his senior CID officer. 'Gemma, you get onto the techs and get them moving. Send Vinny Gillespie out to get a statement from Stewart Dalmer, and for now, Joe, Sheila, I need every scrap of information you can give me on Brenda's movements the last time you saw her.'

Twenty minutes later, Cummins's secretary had taken the necessary details, during which time there had been a couple of phone calls, Gemma returned and Cummins brought them up to speed on the calls.

'The Sanford Gazette has already got hold of the story. Their reporter wouldn't say where it came from, and naturally, Sergeant Earle on reception refused to comment on it. It looks as if we'll have to go public on the matter.'

'Probably one of our members talking out of turn,' Joe commented. 'Alec Staines plays golf with Ian Lofthouse.'

Sheila was more positive. 'There was nothing in the video which said the kidnapper wanted a news blackout, Terry.'

'And that could be worse,' Gemma observed, and when the focus was on her, she went on, 'If he doesn't give a hoot who knows, he won't give a toss what damage he might do to Brenda.'

The remark served only to fuel Joe's increasing frustration. 'Or what he might have already done to her.'

'Joe—'

He cut his niece off. 'You were brought up to tell it like it is, Gemma, not pussyfoot around, and you were the one who first suggested he could have already snuffed her.' He turned on Cummins. 'There must be something we can do,' he repeated.

'I told you. If you've any ideas, I'll listen, but right now, the only thing I can do is try to contain the damage before the Gazette print the story. I'll call the press and TV in and make a statement. I won't tell them about the video message we've had from this clown, and as I said before, you two should keep it to yourselves.'

Joe shook his head 'I'll cut along to the Gazette offices and have a word with Lofthouse. He might not be willing to disclose his sources to you but I can twist his arm in ways you can't. And if it is one of our members...' Joe trailed off and rose to leave but Gemma stopped him.

'Just minute, Joe, Sheila. There is one thing you can do. Slide your brains into gear and think why Brenda would be targeted and why he insists that you should follow his instructions. Not us, but you two.'

'Good point,' Cummins said. 'Not just someone with a grudge against Brenda, but someone harbouring a chip on their shoulder with you, Joe, or you, Sheila.'

'Where Joe's concerned, you could have a queue from here to Leeds.' Sheila gave Joe a wan smile. 'I'm not thinking of your grumpy moods, but the people you've helped put away over the years, Joe.'

'And you're right,' Joe conceded. 'And the queue could stretch a lot further than Leeds. When it comes to Sheila, the only one I can think of is the nutter who tried to kill her the other Christmas.'

'I'll run a check with the prison service, make sure he's still inside,' Cummins said.

'What about the Valentine Strangler.' Sheila said. 'Remember him?'

Joe nodded. 'He held Sheila, me and a CID man at gunpoint in Sheila's place.'

Gemma nodded. 'I remember him. He got life.'

'Run a check, make sure he's still inside too,' Cummins ordered. 'And if that's it, I'd better get a press conference organised.'

'Right enough, Terry. We'll keep you posted.' Joe got to his feet and sat down again. 'Just a minute. You're on about people who might or might not still be inside. What about him you told us about yesterday, Gemma? Him from Yorkshire Jewellers? Atherton, was it?'

She was stunned. 'Hell. I forgot about him.' Gemma addressed her commander. 'Vic Atherton, sir. Joe helped put him away a few years back. Granted leave for his mother's funeral and he absconded.'

'We have an APW out on him?'

'Nationwide, sir. I wouldn't have said he was this dangerous. Reports indicate that he's a lot tougher than when he first went inside, but there's nothing to suggest that he'd do anything like this. We've just warned the public to keep their distance and bell us if they spot him.'

'Nevertheless, that's the kind of thinking we need. Brief our people, Gemma and pile the pressure on.' Cummins gave Joe and Sheila a grim smile. 'Try not to worry. I know that's not easy, but we'll be pulling out all the stops for her.'

Joe nodded. 'All right. We'll leave it with you. Keep us in the loop, though, and if we hear anything more—'

'Which you will,' Gemma interrupted.

'Which we will, we'll let you know.'

From the police station they went into Galleries shopping mall and Ma's Pantry, a favourite port of call for Sheila and Brenda. Joe organised coffee and toast for them, and grumbling about the price, joined Sheila at a window seat.

'Ideas?' he asked.

'Nothing constructive. Only one thing occurred to me. It cannot possibly be… *him*.'

Joe was puzzled, but her stress on the final word told its own story. 'Oh, you mean…' He trailed off. Ever since the attempt on her life, Sheila did not like to hear the man's name.

She pressed an explanation upon him. 'If it was him, he would have come for me, or possibly you considering you're the one who stopped him from ending my life.'

It made a kind of sense, but Joe remained more

cautious. 'It's not safe to eliminate anyone at this stage, Sheila. Terry will check with the prison service. If he's still inside, then fine, but until then let's keep our options open.' He chewed on a bite of cold, rubbery toast and scowled. 'When will these places learn to serve food while it's still hot, or at least warm?'

'Distraction only works so far, Joe and we have more important matters on our plate than cold toast. What are we going to tell Lee, Cheryl, and Kayleigh? Especially Kayleigh. I know she's not the brightest spark in the heavens, but she's a good, honest worker, and she gets on well with Brenda. She'll be very upset.'

Joe washed the toast down with a mouthful of insipid tea, and grimaced again. 'Dishwater.' Bringing his concentration to bear on Sheila's question, he said, 'Terry said he's going to organise the press and TV, that could mean it'll be on the screen in The Lazy Luncheonette. We really need to get back there and speak to them before Cummins shows up on the telly.'

'Soften the blow?'

'Something like that.'

Ten minutes later, they climbed into their cars, and with Joe leading the way, drove out of Sanford, along Doncaster Road and to the parking area behind The Lazy Luncheonette, where they entered through the rear door. It was coming up to half past nine. The draymen were long gone, but the front of the café was busy with the office workers from the floors above, some of them with large-ish orders for their colleagues, others who had just arrived for their day's work.

Joe donned his whites and relieved Cheryl at the counter, Sheila put on her tabard and began assisting Kayleigh with delivering meals while Cheryl assisted her husband, Lee, in the kitchen.

'So where's Auntie Brenda?' Lee asked.

'Later, lad,' Joe said from the counter. 'When we're not so busy.'

In fact, it was almost an hour before business slackened off sufficiently, for Joe and Sheila to commandeer table 5 and call their small crew around them. Joe left the announcement to Sheila. Not that he was shy of delivering bad news, but he guessed that she would express herself more gently than he.

Even so, Cheryl greeted the news with astonishment, Lee frowned as if he were struggling to take it in, and Kayleigh flopped into a seat and burst into tears. Sheila and Cheryl made efforts to console her without much success.

'She's my friend,' Kayleigh wept, 'and she's been really good to me since I came to work here, teaching me how to use stuff like the fancy coffee machine.' She was referring to the barista machine which Joe had had installed to cope with the orders from the offices above them.

Made of sterner stuff than either of the other two women, Joe told Kayleigh, 'Don't you worry about Brenda, lass. We'll get her back, and when we get hold of this nutter, we'll make pies out of what's left of him.'

'And that won't be much,' Sheila said, backing up her boss for once.

# Chapter Six

'I say to this individual, stop this now and give yourself up. As matters stand you are guilty of abduction and attempted extortion. These are serious crimes, but if you should hurt Mrs Jump in any way, the charges will be much more serious, and the inevitable prison sentence which goes with them will be so much longer.'

The moment Chief Superintendent Cummins stopped speaking the assembled press crowd bombarded him with questions.

In the dining area of The Lazy Luncheonette the atmosphere was silent as the grave. Everyone's eyes, staff, diners, the few people queueing at the counter, were riveted on the large screen television fixed to the wall, their attention focused upon Cummins's five-minute address. Even as the press clamoured for answers to their questions, those people present in the café did not stir from their near-catatonic, rapt fixation with the TV screen.

'Can we ask about the lady who has been abducted,' one reporter demanded.

'Brenda Jump is well-known in Sanford,' Cummins replied. 'A long-serving member of the community, she's treasurer of the Sanford 3rd Age Club. I have to confess that she's also a personal friend. I've known Brenda and her colleagues at The Lazy Luncheonette ever since my days as a community constable in Sanford. I'm compelled to put aside my personal feelings in this matter, and in respect of that, I've called our local headquarters in Leeds to bring in a senior officer who will treat this matter dispassionately. That doesn't mean to say I'm standing down. Responsibility for law and order in this town falls upon me, and I will not shy away from that responsibility purely because I'm familiar with the victim.'

'Well said, Terry,' Joe commented from behind the counter. He half turned towards his kitchen staff. 'Right, come on. We've got people here to feed.' He turned again and focused on his next customer. 'What can I do you for, luv?'

The café slowly came alive again, and over the next hour the staff were too busy to concentrate on what had happened to one of their friends, but as that hour passed, Joe noticed a gathering outside the premises. Press, he guessed, but he also noticed people amongst the crowd who were dressed in overalls of one description or another. George Robson was plain to see, so too was his best friend, Owen Frickley, and he could also see Barry Standish, one of Sanford Brewery's leading draymen, and one of Joe's primary antagonists during the breakfast period.

It was Barry who fought his way through the press crowd and into the café. He ignored the queue, and made his way to the counter. 'Is this all for real, Joe?'

Joe tutted. 'No. Terry Cummins set it all up as a trailer for a new police series. Course it's true, you barmpot. Now bugger off. I've got people to serve.'

'Well, when you've got a minute, shove me a cuppa, and I'll speak to you when you're not busy.'

Joe poured two beakers of tea, one of which he passed to Barry, the other to his customer. 'Sorry about that, luv. But he and his mates are here for breakfast every morning, and they know Brenda really well.' He tallied up the woman's bill. 'Call it eight-fifty for cash.'

She handed over the money. 'It must be good to know that you've got so many friends willing to turn out for her, Joe.'

Joe gave her change. 'She's a popular lass is our Brenda, and a lot of people in this town will be seriously piddled off with the bloke that's nabbed her.'

The woman tutted and picked up her tea. 'I've heard about Brenda. Just goes to show, don't it? You have got to be a bit careful who you're letting your knickers down for.'

Joe was still pondering this jaundiced view of Brenda when the rush died off half an hour later and he could join Sheila and Barry at table 5. Brenda had a reputation as a "merry widow" and it was true to say that she dated a number of different man, but she did not sleep around.

Sheila had already given Barry the overview, and the drayman took a positive view of the matter. 'Right, listen, me and the guys are out and about round Sanford, Wakefield, Pontefract, just about everywhere every day.' He glanced at his watch. 'I've about another two hours before I'm due back at the brewery. I'll call the lads together before we knock off, and tell them to keep their eyes peeled for any sign of Brenda or the scrote what's bagged her. If we get our hands on him, Joe, there won't be a lot left for the filth to prosecute.'

Joe was pleased to hear it, although in truth he expected nothing less from the café's most faithful patrons. 'Only trouble is, Barry, nobody knows what he looks like and we haven't a clue where he's holding Brenda.'

Barry was nonplussed. 'Oh. I never thought of that. Still and all, we'll keep our eyes and ears open.'

Sheila reached across the table and took his hand. 'That's what we like to hear, Barry. We're grateful for your support, and if you get to know anything at all, whether through work, or when you're out and about socialising, don't hesitate to give us a ring. Joe and I will be working closely with the police until this is sorted out.'

Joe scribbled his mobile number on a piece of paper and slid it across the table. 'My phone's on 24/7, mate. If you learn anything, you or any of your mates, give me a shout.'

'Count on it.' Barry drained his beaker. 'Time I weren't here. I'll see you for breakfast tomorrow morning.'

As he left, fighting his way through the reporters on the pavement, Joe got to his feet. 'Terry's not the only one who needs to deal with the press. I'll be with them for a minute or two, Sheila. After that, as long as Lee, Cheryl, and Kayleigh can cope, what say we shoot into town and hassle Ian Lofthouse?'

'See where he got the story from?' Sheila asked, and Joe nodded.

Because there was so little Joe could tell them,

the task of dealing with the press pack took only a few minutes. After that, a brief word with the three assistants allowed him and Sheila to climb into his car for the short journey into Sanford, and by half past one, they were seated opposite Ian Lofthouse in the Sanford Gazette building.

A little older than Joe and Sheila, Lofthouse had been the managing editor of the newspaper for the last decade, and he had an alternating, friendly and fractious relationship with Joe. Amicable when Joe brought him news or advertising revenue for the 3rd Age Club, less so when Joe was in trouble and the Gazette reported on it. Now, however, he floundered, sympathetic but obdurate in refusing to name the source of the story despite the pressure both Joe and Sheila put him under.

'This is us you're talking to, Ian,' Sheila reminded him. 'Brenda is our best friend, she's in trouble, her life is under threat.'

'Journalistic privilege, Sheila. I'm sorry, but—'

Joe cut him off. 'Not good enough. When that bag, Ecclesfield slagged me off during the Valentine Strangler business, who fed you the full story when it was all over? Me.'

'Yes, but I didn't name you, Joe.'

'You damn well did.'

'No. It was the cops who named you.'

Joe ignored the rejoinder. 'And when Ray Dockerty walled me up for murdering Vaughan, who gave you the real tale when I was proven innocent?'

'Again, I didn't name you, Dockerty and the

courts did. And anyway, it's not like your life was under threat, was it?'

'Mine was the other Christmas,' Sheila pointed out, 'and we gave you the in-depth after it was all over. Now come on, Ian, who told you about Brenda? Was it Alec Staines?'

'Alec?'

'We know you play golf with him,' Joe pointed out.

'No. It wasn't Alec. In fact, it wasn't any of your 3rd Age Club clowns.'

'Then tell us who.'

Lofthouse hedged. He half turned in his seat and gazed out through the window over Market Square. At length, he turned back. 'The filth already know this, Joe, so I might as well tell you. Your Gemma was round before Terry Cummins went on TV. That video you and Sheila received, well we got a copy of it too. Padded envelope, no postmark, hand delivered sometime in the early hours, and before you ask, no we don't have CCTV covering the front entrance. Well, we do, but it's inside, and our mailbox is on the wall outside. When Gemma came, we handed the video and the envelope to her.'

Joe and Sheila exchanged a cautious glance. 'He obviously doesn't care who knows,' Sheila said.

'Correct,' Lofthouse agreed. 'And let's face it, that doesn't sound good for Brenda, does it?'

Joe and Sheila stood, ready to leave. 'Do us a favour, Ian,' Joe pleaded. 'If you get anything else, anything at all, gave us a bell as well as the filth.'

'Are you willing to give me the full SP when

43

it's all over?'

'Of course,' Sheila said.

'In that case, you've got a deal.'

* * *

From the Gazette offices, they walked to Gale Street and the police station, where they joined Cummins and Gemma in the chief superintendent's office.

'We just wondered whether anything else had come in, Terry,' Joe said.

'Nothing, Joe. Sorry. Chances are you and Sheila – and Lofthouse at the Gazette – will get to know things before we do.' He glanced across at Gemma. 'Do you have anything to add?'

'A couple of things, sir. The Valentine Strangler is still in prison, so it's not him. Same applies to the scrote who tried to poison Sheila. It can't be either of them… or put it this way, it can't be either of them directly. That's not to say that they don't have someone working on the outside. Problem is, we don't know what this toerag's demanding, do we? I mean, for all we know, he could demand that we get either of those two lags released.'

Joe shook his head. 'That's a nonstarter, Gemma. Brenda said that it was down to me and Sheila, not you guys. How could we arrange for anyone to be released from prison? No, if they're still inside, then they're not involved.'

Cummins laid down the law. 'We're not eliminating any possibilities just yet. You're right, Joe, it's unlikely that he wants either of them released, but we're keeping all options open. Just so you both know, I've asked Ray Dockerty to take control of the enquiry. He'll be with us first thing in the morning. Fact of the matter is, Gemma and I are too close to this. We both know Brenda too well, and I don't want the enquiry coloured by any personal feelings we may have.'

'Mr Dockerty knows Brenda too,' Sheila said. 'Perhaps not as well as you and Gemma, but we have met on several occasions.'

'No, I think they're right, Sheila,' Joe said. 'It's true that Ray Dockerty knows Brenda, but not half as well as Terry and Gemma do. And we know Ray, don't we? Like Terry, he won't let personal feelings get in the way.' He took out his tobacco tin and began to roll a cigarette. 'Have you been in touch with Vic Atherton's ex-wife yet?'

Gemma answered. 'Yes. And she insists she hasn't seen anything of him and if she had, she'd bubble him right away.'

The cigarette completed, Joe dropped it in his shirt pocket for later consumption. 'I don't know what else we can do for now, so Sheila and I will clear off back to The Lazy Luncheonette and wait for developments.'

'Good enough,' Cummins agreed. 'Remember, both of you. Anything at all. It doesn't matter how tiny, insignificant, how trivial, give us a shout. The entire station is on full alert, and we have an ARU on standby in Leeds. If we get one sniff of this guy, they can be here in twenty minutes.'

Sheila fretted. 'My only concern with that, Terry, is that if this man is confronted with armed police officers, he may very well decide to take Brenda with him.'

'We know that, Sheila. Trust me, our people are not that trigger happy. They'll be under strict fire control orders. Our intention is to bring this business to a peaceful end without any harm coming to Brenda or the idiot who's holding her.'

# Chapter Seven

He called every two to three hours, usually to let her use the slop bucket and to feed her now and then. The timing was a guesstimate. Along with her rings, he'd removed her wristwatch, an expensive, 40th birthday gift from her late husband, leaving her with no idea of the time.

The cold, too, had begun to get to her. She had been held captive in this dire place for… she with no external lighting to hint at the passing of day and night, she did not know how long, but she guessed two or three days, she was wearing only thin clothing, the same dinner dress she wore for her date with Stewart Dalmer on Monday evening, and the danger of hypothermia frequently came to haunt her. She was no expert on the subject, but she was aware of some of the early symptoms. Shivering, pale and cold skin, fast breathing, tiredness. She also knew that if and when it set in, it would clog up her thinking and speech, and she could not afford for that to happen.

Fortunately, her captor had realised it too. On his first visit of the day (which day, Brenda still did not know) he brought a small two-bar, electric heater, plugged it into a wall socket and switched it on.

With an evil chuckle, he said, 'Can't have you freezing to death, can we, Jump? I'm reserving that pleasure for myself.'

It was not particularly effective, although it did

stave off the worst of the chill, but it also provided Brenda with an unexpected bonus, one the man had never considered. It bathed the entire room in soft, orange light, and that enabled her to focus properly on the information boards around her, and to finalise her plans.

Aside from his semi-jocular threat on delivering the heater, whenever he turned up, he said little or nothing. He did not need to. Brenda could see the jagged-edged hunting knife slipped into his belt, close to his right hip where he could withdraw and apply it.

Although much of her terror had dissipated, she was still afraid of him, afraid of what he might do, so she co-operated. And between his visits, she concentrated on those boards, suppressing her anxiety, forcing her mind and memory to work, absorb the information she was taking in, not only learning, but memorising it.

And at those times when she was not actively engaged upon the project, she considered the method of delivery. He would notice. She was certain he would. How could she persuade him that there was nothing untoward in her actions, that it was an innocuous aspect of… Aspect of what? It was not until he returned with the video camera and tablet, and beamed a powerful light into her eyes that the logical answer occurred to her.

He arrived again, set up his camera, and with it running, he approached her, and her terror reached new heights as he pressed the hunting knife to her throat.

'Please,' she wept. 'Don't. I'm begging you…'

He said nothing, but drew the blade across her neck, and puzzlement enveloped her. She could feel the flow of… Blood? But that was impossible. She did not feel the cut and there was no pain.

He returned to the camera, held up the tablet and showed it to her. 'Read.'

Brenda focused her eyes on the tablet screen. 'That was a theatrical knife with fake blood. Unless you follow these instructions to the letter, next time it will be the real thing.'

She longed to say more. She yearned to express her dread, but she dare not. She knew that if she tried, he would cut her off, and with one eye on the real hunting knife still lodged in his belt at the right hip, there was the ever present danger that he would cut her, full stop.

He switched screens and as new information appeared, ready for Brenda to read, she reminded herself of her plan. This man was seriously unhinged and she had no doubt that he would not hesitate to terminate her life. Now was the time for her courage to come to the fore.

As she began to read the instructions, she went into her plan.

# Chapter Eight

Along with Joe, Sheila, Gemma, and Cummins himself, Ray Dockerty was in attendance when they gathered in the chief superintendent's small office on Friday morning.

Detective Superintendent Dockerty had crossed paths with Joe on a number of occasions, the worst of which was when he remanded Joe on suspicion of murder. A huge man in every sense of the word, he was blunt and outspoken, yet intelligent enough not to rush to hasty conclusions. Indeed, during the episode when he brought Joe before the courts it was only after the evidence pointed him in that direction, and when Joe was demonstrated to be innocent, Dockerty attended the remand prison in person to bring Joe home.

Both Joe and Sheila (and Ian Lofthouse at the Sanford Gazette) had received video recordings on familiar USB sticks the previous day, and reached agreement with Gemma to bring them to the police station first thing Friday.

Gathered in Cummins's office, before they could get down to business, Joe opened proceedings with a query. 'Any news on Vic Atherton, Gemma?'

It was Dockerty who responded. 'We're on it right across the county, Joe, but frankly. We have more to worry about with Brenda Jump's abduction.'

'So you don't think it could be him?'

'I told you yesterday, it's not really his style,' Gemma said.

Joe waved a flaccid hand at Cummins. 'Terry also told us not to dismiss anything.'

'And we're not discounting him,' Cummins responded. 'Merely saying that he's unlikely. Now can we get on?'

Gemma ran the video and everyone cringed when the fake knife slid across Brenda's throat. Joe and Sheila were inured to the shock. Both had watched the recordings in their homes the previous night.

Brenda appeared terrified but nevertheless focused on the message she was compelled to deliver. 'That was a theatrical knife with fake blood. Unless you follow his instructions to the letter, next time it will be the real thing.' There was a blunt cut to the video, and with her eyes blinking rapidly, she began to read the main message. 'The demand is simple. Twenty-five thousand pounds in various denominations, to be parcelled up in a plain paper bag, the kind you get from supermarkets and other High Street shops. Instructions for delivery of the money will follow, and it will be delivered by Joe Murray. No one else. If there are any police in the vicinity of the drop, the money will not be collected, but my life will be forfeit.' She was obviously struggling to control her emotions. 'Please. I'm begging you. Follow the instructions to the letter.'

The video ended with the fake knife held up before the camera lens.

Holding court, Cummins passed the buck to

Dockerty who shrugged. 'Not much I can say at this stage, Terry.' He looked beyond the station commander. 'Gemma, did the video teams get anywhere with their enhancements?'

'Very little, sir. They say the perp focusses the camera too close to Brenda for them to see enough of the background to enable even an educated guess. All they will say is it's some kind of concrete structure with no windows to the outside. It could be anything from a nuclear bunker to the underground access point of a reservoir or sewage works. If it's the latter, Brenda could be held in the Sanford area, but if it's a nuclear bunker, or something of that nature, she could be anywhere in the country but for Sanford.' She smiled and winced. 'We're not exactly a first strike target, so we don't have any nuclear bunkers round here.'

Dockerty shrugged. 'Okay. Let's get teams out to the reservoirs and sewage plants in the Leeds-stroke-Wakefield-stroke-Sanford area.' He turned to Joe and Sheila. 'Do you have anything to add?'

Sheila shook her head, but Joe had more to say. 'Well, yeah. Have you noticed how much Brenda is blinking?'

'Oh, that's the light, Joe,' Sheila said. 'I think he's keeping her in the dark most of the time and when he shines that lamp in her face, it—'

'Yeah, I thought so too,' Joe interrupted, 'but as we've watched it again, I'm not so sure.' He took in all of them with his gaze. 'I'm just wondering if she's trying to get a message to us.'

The suggestion met with smiles. 'Come off it, Joe,' Cummins said. 'You and she have been cosying up since... I can't remember when, and considering her reputation with men—'

Once again, Joe interrupted. 'And you think fluttering her eyelashes would be on her mind while she's tied up and walled up with a nutter?'

'Keep your cool, Joe,' Dockerty suggested. 'Let's run it again and see what you're talking about.'

He took the remote and set the video playing. Right away they could see what Joe was talking about and they watched as Brenda began to speak, but this time focused on her eyelids as they spelled out: blink-blink-blink, blinker-blinker-blinker, blink-blink-blink.

'Y'see,' Joe declared. 'Dot, dot, dot, dash, dash, dash, dot, dot, dot. SOS. It's Morse code.'

Dockerty laughed. 'That's daft. Why would she send out an SOS? We already know she needs help.'

Joe would not be persuaded. 'She's not putting it out as a mayday. That's her way of telling us she's using code. And if you run the rest of it, you'll see she keeps on doing it.'

Sheila kept her voice soft, persuasive. 'Joe, with the best will in the world, I know Brenda better than anyone does. There's no way she's familiar with Morse code. SOS, yes, but good lord, we all know that particular code, don't we? Other than that, I'm sorry, but she can't do what you're suggesting.'

Joe fought back. 'And I say you're wrong. All of you. She's trying to tell us something, and it's more than SOS. Watch the rest of it and see if I'm not right.'

Dockerty aimed the remote and set the video running again.

As it progressed Joe's idea become clearer but if Brenda was signalling with her eyelids, it meant nothing to anyone in the room.

'We'd better get it checked out, Terry,' Dockerty said to Cummins. 'I mean I'm not saying Joe's got it right, but there is something odd about it. Maybe Mrs Riley's right and it's the intensity of the light he's shining in her eyes, but we need to know. I'll get it off to Leeds and tell them to pull a specialist in.'

Joe frowned. 'Why Leeds? I thought the police all learned Morse.'

'What century are you living in, Joe?' Gemma asked. 'I never learned it.'

'But—'

Cummins cut Joe off. 'Technology. We have other ways of communicating these days.'

Joe huffed out his breath. 'Sending this thing off to Leeds could take hours. Days even, and Brenda's—'

'Do you have any other ideas?' Dockerty interrupted. 'Do you know Morse?'

'He only knows the TV detective,' Sheila commented.

'You're right,' Joe admitted, 'but I think I know a man who does and he's here in Sanford.' He took out his smartphone and dialled.

\* \* \*

At the rank of Captain, Les Tanner had been a member of the Territorial Army Reserve for many years before he retired from the service. Head of payroll at Sanford town hall, he had also been a founder member of the Sanford 3rd Age Club along with his lady friend, now partner, Sylvia Goodson. In that capacity, he'd also been a longstanding critic of Joe Murray's administrative inefficiency, an example of which materialised when Joe rang him. 'Office hours, Murray? We're not all like you, you know. Some of us don't enjoy the luxury of doing as we please, when it suits us.'

'Neither do I. I have customers and they come first.'

'Along with a shedload of insults,' Tanner retorted.

'For God's sake shut up and listen will you? Can you read Morse code?'

'Why?'

'Because if you can, get over to Gale Street and check into Terry Cummins's office. We need you here.'

'I'm in the middle of a morning's work, man.'

'Watching a pen trace its way across a sheet of paper? That's not work. Now, listen to me, Les, this is important.'

'I—'

'You could be saving Brenda's life.'

Joe's announcement worked. It stopped Tanner in the act of protesting that he couldn't do it and when he next spoke, he was more contingent. 'I'm a little rusty, but I'll be there in, say, ten minutes. Ask Mr Cummins to get the kettle on.'

\*\*\*

By the time Tanner arrived and was furnished with tea, Joe had his explanation prepared. 'These buggers, Terry, Ray, Gemma, and Sheila don't believe me, Les, but I'm certain Brenda is trying to get a message to us. When you watch the video, forget the background, forget Brenda's fear, forget how grubby she is, forget what she's saying, just focus on the way she blinks.'

'Do us all a favour, Murray, and go back to your café. I know what I'm doing.'

'That'll make a change,' Joe grumbled and left Tanner to it.

'Is he really that good?' Dockerty asked as they vacated the small office Tanner had been allocated.

Joe's response was scathing. 'A bloody toy soldier Territorial. If you listen to him, he accepted the German surrender at the end of the last war, and that was years before he was born. Yes, and he blames me for World War Two, and it was even more years before I was born.' Joe glanced back into the office where Tanner was watching the video and consulting a printout of Morse code. 'But to be fair, Ray, he knows this kind of stuff even if he does need a reminder, and he's a good club member. He cares about Brenda, like we all do. If I'm right, he'll crack the message Brenda is trying to send us.'

Dockerty laughed. 'If you're right, I'll stand drinks all round in the nearest pub.'

\*\*\*

'I have to hand it to you, Joe, I believe you were right, but the message doesn't make much sense.' Tanner placed his sheet on the desk before Cummins who read it and passed it round. As it reached Joe, he read, NURZEAK ZUAKEG.

'Garbage,' Joe declared. 'Typical Brenda when she's sunk a few Camparis.'

The comment raised a chuckle but not from Sheila. 'Really, Joe, that's not very helpful.' She took in the rest of the room. 'I'm sorry, but I think we have this wrong. Colin – her late husband – was a manager at Sanford Main Colliery. He wouldn't need to understand Morse code to do his job, and I insist that Brenda never learned it. Why would she?'

Silence fell as each descended into their own thoughts. At length, Cummins broke it. 'Coincidence then. Nice try, Joe, and obviously, we're grateful but—'

'No. Hang on a minute,' Joe interrupted. He focussed on Tanner. 'Les, how accurate is your interpretation?'

'Spot on. I know what I'm doing.'

'And I accept that. Sheila, you say Brenda doesn't know Morse. So where did she get the idea, and more important, where did she learn it?' Scanning the room, his eyes burned into them. 'She's tied to that damn chair, she can't even turn round. Not that it'd do her much good because according to Gemma there's nothing on the wall behind her, so whatever prompted the idea must be in front of her, staring her in the face. And looking at the lighting, our man has put some kind of heater in there for her, which means she must be able to see fairly well. Now where would you find a printout of Morse code pinned to a wall?'

Tanner answered without hesitation. 'A military communications centre or a nuclear bunker.'

Joe gave him a small round of applause. 'Exactly. Now tell me this, Les. Bearing in mind Brenda doesn't know Morse, considering she's faced with a nutter, is it possible that she got some of the dots and dashes wrong?'

'Entirely possible.' Tanner picked up his interpretation and made a study of it. 'Twice Brenda has signalled the letter Z, which is very close to…' He trailed off to study his printout of Morse code. 'L and B as matter of fact. See here.' He turned the printout to face them. 'L is dot-dash-dot-dot. Z, which is what Brenda has signalled, is dash-dash-dot-dot. Similarly, B is dash-dot-dot-dot. If she got the signals slightly wrong, then either of them would come through as Z. On that basis, translating her message again, the first word now reads, either NURLEAK or NURBEAK, and given that C – dash-dot-dash-dot – is not that far removed from R – dot-dash-dot – and R is not too far removed from K – dash-dot-dash instead of dot-dash-dot, we could reasonable translate that first word as NUCLEAR.' Tanner tapped his original translation. 'With that in mind, translating the odd errors in the second word, would render the word "bunker", and the whole message now reads, "nuclear bunker".'

His tedious, point by point analysis was greeted with silence.

Gemma broke it. 'That let's Sanford out then. We have no nuclear bunkers. And, if he bagged her late on Monday night, he could be anywhere in the country.'

'You mean he and she could,' Joe corrected her, and then promptly shot his niece down. 'No, girl, I'm sorry, but you're wrong. He's here in Sanford.'

Dockerty frowned. 'How do you work that out, Joe?'

'Brenda said he wants me to deliver the ransom. You think he's gonna drag me all over the country? Face, it, he'll keep tabs on me, and he'll be monitoring the drop point. Send me to the home counties or somewhere like that where they have these bunkers, and he wouldn't know whether it was me or someone else driving, and if he lost me in the traffic, he'd be up the creek without one.'

'You have a point,' Sheila agreed, 'but in truth, he'd be more concerned for you getting lost.' To the whole group, she said, 'I think Joe is right. We don't know where he's holding Brenda, but the drop will be here in Sanford, or at the very worst, Leeds or Wakefield. Somewhere Joe knows well.'

Cummins looked to Dockerty who shrugged. 'It hurts me to say this, Terry, but I think Joe and Sheila may be right and it looks like it's gonna cost me a pint all round.' He smiled to show he was only joking at their expense. 'I do have other observations, the first of which is, would Brenda know what the inside of a nuclear bunker looks like?'

'With the possible exception of Les, I don't

think any of us would,' Joe responded, 'but like Les said, what other kind of building would have something pinned to the wall that spelled out Morse code? You heard Sheila, and I agree with her. There's no way that Brenda would have any knowledge of Morse code, so it has to be something on those walls that gave her the idea, and also gave her the code. To me, that indicates a military building.' He switched his attention to Tanner. 'Would you agree with that, Les?'

'I already said so, Joe. Working on the assumption that Brenda really is sending us signals by Morse code – and personally, like Joe, I have no doubt – then I would agree with Joe. She is being held in some kind of military building, and given that there appeared to be no windows, it has to be some kind of communication centre. A nuclear bunker would be favourite.' Now he turned to Joe. 'But as Gemma has already pointed out, there are no nuclear bunkers in this area.'

'And you know that for a fact, do you Les?' Dockerty asked.

'Of course not. Remember, I was a comparatively junior officer, a captain. The true location of nuclear bunkers has always been a closely guarded secret.' Now he concentrated on Cummins and Dockerty. 'I don't doubt that we have this right, gentlemen, and if you'll take my advice, you'll get onto the MoD, get them to send someone in who knows precisely what he's talking about.'

Cummins, who had taken only a small part in the discussion, let out an exasperated sigh. 'We're stretched to the limit with general policing, and now

I have to call on the bloody army to tell us where we might find a kidnap victim. It's days like this that tempt me to ask for my pension.'

Joe let out a humourless chuckle. 'Maybe it's time you joined the 3rd Age Club, Terry.'

Cummins sneered. 'I'm not that desperate.'

# Chapter Nine

It was coming up to twelve noon when Joe and Sheila got back to The Lazy Luncheonette. They quickly removed their outer clothing, donned their workwear, and while Sheila took over the delivery of orders from Kayleigh, Joe manned the counter, facing a queue which stretched back to the entrance and beyond.

Outside, many of them pacing back and forth across the pavement, the press were still gathered in numbers.

'They've been there all morning, Joe,' Cheryl told him. 'I've told them, there's nothing more we know, but it's worse than talking to you when you're in a bad mood.'

'Thanks for that vote of confidence, Cheryl. I'll deal with them once the rush is over. Until then, they can pi—'

'Joe!' Sheila's warning cut him off.

'I was going to say, piddle off.'

Cheryl laughed and then her face became more serious. 'Even our Danny's asking what's happened to Auntie Brenda. He's worried about her.'

'I've telled our Cheryl to keep lying to him,' Lee called from the kitchen.

The woman herself looked downcast. 'And I don't like having to do that.'

Joe smiled. 'Just tell him Uncle Joe's on the case and our Brenda will be okay.'

Outside on the pavement what appeared to be

some kind of scuffle had broken out, and Joe was about to go out there and break it up, when the burly figure of George Robson, and his best friend, Owen Frickley, appeared in the doorway, and gave him a cheery wave.

It was almost ten minutes before the pair reached the counter, and ordered the Friday special, battered cod served with chips and mushy peas.

'Any news on Brenda, Joe?' George asked.

'Yep, and it's all bad. Don't bother asking, George, because we don't know. The cops know everything we know, and Terry Cummins will brief the press later on.'

Owen, taller, slimmer, fitter and more muscular than his friend, pointed a finger at George. 'This dipstick's still convinced that it's Dalmer.'

'Yeah, well, George never did like Stewart, did he?' Joe took George's money, gave change, and went on, 'Get it into your head, George. It's nothing to do with anyone in the 3rd Age Club.'

'You'd better be right, Joe, cause if I find out it is Dalmer, there won't be a lot left of him by the time I hand him over to the cops.'

Joe gestured at the never-ending queue. 'Stop talking like a prat and get outta the way. I've other customers waiting to be served… Oh. Wait. Tell you what, George, can you meet me in the Miners Arms about half seven, eight o'clock tonight? You and Owen?'

The two men shrugged. 'No prob, Joe,' Owen agreed. 'What's to do?'

'I'll tell you when I get there.'

Under normal circumstances, the lunchtime

rush would be over by half past one, two o'clock, but with news of Brenda spreading around the town, The Lazy Luncheonette had suddenly become one of the most popular venues in Sanford. Amongst the huge queue, a good number of the massed shoppers visiting the Sanford Retail Park, readily identified by the logos on their shopping bags, were calling to the café, all of which meant the queue was there until turned three o'clock, and were it not for the worry of Brenda's situation, Joe would have been rubbing his hands with avaricious glee.

At four o'clock, the cleaning over and done with, they closed the door for the last time, and Sheila pulled Joe. 'You're meeting George and Owen in the Miners Arms?'

'Something that occurred to me when they were here screaming at lunchtime. They might know more than we do, but we were too busy to speak to them.'

'Do you need me there for moral support?'

'Not particularly. Hell, it's George and Owen I'm dealing with. Come along if you like, but to be honest, Sheila, you look shattered. You might be better off taking a night away from it all.'

She sighed. 'I don't know whether I can get away from it. How many years have we known each other, Joe? Half a century. Ever since the schoolyard. The three of us are like Dumas's musketeers. All for one and one for all. Even when we fall out it's never for very long, is it?'

Joe chuckled. 'Three musketeers. I like that. More like three serverteers, but it's appropriate. How many times have you and Brenda got me out of a mess, whether with the law or whatever?'

'Like the time we took you off to Torremolinos after the fake heart attack?'

'And when Denise was killed, you dragged me off to Palmanova.'

'And I will never forget what you did when that maniac tried to poison me. We went to Tenerife to get over that, didn't we?'

Joe nodded. 'We did. So where will we go when we get Brenda back?'

'Benidorm?'

'Now that sounds like a plan.'

'But we have Bridlington planned.'

'Planned but not booked.' He tapped the side of his nose. 'Leave it to me. 'I'll get the members to change their minds.'

Sheila smiled again. 'You're a lovely man on the quiet, Joe Murray.'

'Yes, but don't tell everyone that. I have a grumpy reputation to live up to.'

Sheila left and Joe did not know whether he would see her in the Miners Arms that evening, but he did know what he had to do now. Gently, carefully, he peeled away the adhesive tape fixing the wanted poster to the window, laid the notice flat on a table, took out his smartphone, and photographed it. After checking that the image was fine, he retrieved the roll of adhesive tape from a drawer behind the counter and pinned the notice back to the window.

'Now we'll see what we can see,' he said to the empty café.

\* \* \*

It was a curious anomaly that while most pubs enjoyed their busiest night on Friday and Saturday evenings, when it came to the Miners Arms, that did not apply. Thanks to the Sanford 3rd Age Club and their weekly disco, Wednesday evening was the pub's busiest.

Joe was in the lounge bar a couple of minutes before eight, and securing a glass of lager, indulged landlord, Mick Chadwick's queries regarding Brenda.

'No progress, then, Joe?'

'Not so you'd notice, Mick.'

'We're all on your side, you know.'

'And we'll be sure to tell Brenda when we get her back.'

*If we get her back.* Joe could not help the negative thought rushing into his head.

looking around the busy room, he spotted George and Owen in a corner table and made his way across to join them.

'You could have brought us a top up,' George complained as Joe sat opposite.

'I can't afford it. I've told you before, I'm a poor man. It's what comes of giving away free teas and meals to tightwads like you.'

Owen laughed. 'All the years I've been calling at your place, Joe, I've never yet had any free nosh.'

George brought them to order. 'Anyway, never mind the patter. Get to the point, Joe. We've a night's beer to get through. What do you want?'

Joe took out his smartphone. 'Get your phones

out, Bluetooth on. I've a picture for you.'

George smacked his lips. 'Your Ali showing everything at her place in Tenerife?'

'Just shut it, George. This is serious stuff.'

The two men followed Joe's instructions, took out their phones, set up Bluetooth, and Joe spent a moment pairing with them, after which he sent his image of the wanted poster to both.

George, ever the leader of the pair, screwed up his face. 'A bloody wanted poster? What are you playing—'

Joe cut him off. 'Vic Atherton. You know him?'

George shook his head. 'Never heard of him.'

Owen was more forthcoming. 'I knew him. Worked at Yorkshire Jewellers until a coupla years ago. Then he got sent down for thieving… Come to think, Joe, you were the one who nailed him, weren't you?'

'That's right. If you read the poster, he's on the run. Now, the cops don't seriously consider him as a candidate for bagging Brenda. I'm not so generous. He has a beef against me and it's possible that he's using Brenda to get back at me.' Joe focused on George. 'I'm surprised you don't know him. All right, he's younger than us, but you're the man about town, George. You're the one who knows everyone.'

George took a healthy swallow of his beer. 'Not really, Joe. Fair enough, I know most of the women, and I know the blokes who'd like to take me apart because I've given their wives, ex-wives, and such, the time of their life. But this geezer…

Sorry, but like I said, I've never heard of him. Was he married?'

Joe nodded, and in stark contrast to George's guzzling, took a delicate sip of his lager. 'He was divorced, or heading in that direction, and it was costing him a fortune. That's why he nicked that ring from Yorkshire Jewellers. Him and his bit on the side, a woman named Fiona Watson. She's been dead about a year, and he married her just before she clocked out.'

'I knew her as well,' Owen said. 'Good looking lass. Relative of the girl who works for you, Kayleigh.'

'Her aunt,' Joe agreed. 'Anyway, to get back to what I was saying, Atherton's on the run. According to our Gemma, his missus will bubble him the minute she claps eyes on him, and I wouldn't argue about that because I don't know the woman. Name of Debbie, and that's as much as I know. But—'

'Debbie Atherton,' George interrupted with a gleeful smile. 'Well, Debbie Hawkridge before she got married. Hell, I remember her. A real goer when she were younger.' A lascivious grin spread across his face. 'She's fair lively now, an' all.'

Joe frowned. 'Let me get this straight. You know the woman as she is now?'

George took a moment to think the matter through. 'Lemme see. It must be about a year or eighteen months since I last saw her. I bumped into her in The Fettlers, we had a couple of drinks, and before you knew it... Well, you know me, you know what I'm like.'

Owen laughed, and Joe tutted his disapproval.

'You never bloody change, do you?'

'It's what life's all about, Joe. As you'd know if you weren't tied to that café of yours.'

Joe dragged the subject back to where it should be. 'So you knew the woman, but you didn't know her husband?'

'Nope. Why would I? She didn't know my ex-wife, and we weren't really interested in either of them. All as I knew, Joe, was that she was divorced. As far as I was concerned, that was the green light.'

Joe switched his attention to Owen. 'I assume you've had the pleasure of her as well, have you?'

Owen shook his head. 'I don't only follow tubby, you know. I do have me own contacts.'

Like a spectator at a tennis rally, Joe's head switched back to George. 'You only saw her the once and you've no idea of her attitude to her ex?'

'Like I said, Joe, we didn't talk about exes. And no, I didn't just see her once. I'd a few dates with her, and by then, she was getting on my wick. Always moaning about the cost of living and being short of money and stuff. Funny, really, cos she worked for a living. It's not like she was on the dole or anything.' George took another slug from his glass. 'You don't think she's hiding her ex from the filth, do you?'

'No, that's not what I'm saying. I'm just wondering if she knows enough about Vic to say whether or not he'd be capable of kidnapping Brenda and holding her to ransom. Have you got an address for her?'

'Have I hell as like. I took her back to my drum every time we met, and when she left the following morning, she took a taxi or bus or something.'

Owen laughed. 'He's always like that, Joe. His generosity is underwhelming.'

'They've already had the benefit of me, haven't they?' George protested.

Joe drank his lager. 'All right. We'll leave it at that. But you two are out and about all the time, and you've got pictures of Vic Atherton so if you clap eyes on him, give me a shout.' He got up, ready to leave.

George rattled his glass on the table. 'Hey, don't we get a drink out of this or something?'

Joe tutted, dug out his wallet, and threw a fiver on the table. 'Just remember, you're not doing this for freebies. You're doing it for Brenda.'

# Chapter Ten

Hot, Mediterranean sunshine blazed from a cloudless sky. The soft and distant lapping of the sea against the shore filled her ears, and the feel of soft sand beneath her heightened the sensations of love coursing through her.

'You know you're the only man for me, don't you? There'll never be anyone else.'

Colin turned to face her, removed his mirror-finish sunglasses and beamed that special smile upon her, the smile that lit up his dark blue eyes. 'I'm the luckiest man alive, Bren, because I have you.'

She craned her neck and kissed him. When she broke away, Joe's smile had gone, replaced by his business-oriented face of determination. 'We don't have time to laze around like this, girl. We've a café to run.'

She returned her most seductive smile. 'Take it easy, Joe. Just enjoy the moment.'

George tried to inject some lusty persuasion into his voice. 'I've got some really special moments in mind, lass.'

Brenda closed her eyes and allowed her imagination to drift.

'I've seen a piece of Royal Doulton I wouldn't mind taking a closer look at,' Stewart said.

'You're sure you don't want to take a closer look at me?'

'Well, I suppose if we can classify antique as

meaning anything over fifty years old, you'd qualify.'

'Brenda's not an antique,' George argued.

'And she has work to do,' Joe insisted.

'When you're through this is my wife you're talking about,' Colin snapped.

'The wife you went and died on?' Joe argued.

'Some husband you were,' George echoed.

Brenda felt her anger rising. That last remark was out of order. Nobody spoke about her beloved Colin like that.

Determined to give them all a piece of her mind, her eyes snapped open… to be greeted by the near darkness and barren squalor of her cell.

She was not sleeping. Not in the accepted sense of the word. With her more acute senses coming to the fore, she realised she was delirious. How long had she been held prisoner in this hell hole? How much longer before her captor collected his ransom and freed her?

The unyielding rigidity of her bindings had caused her pain since… forever really. With nothing to vary the glow of the heater and the thin light of the overhead bulb she had little concept of time, so she could have been locked in this position – his visits and the accompanying breaks excepted – for two days, four days, a week, two weeks. On those occasions when he freed her so she could eat or use the slop bucket, her leg muscles felt weak, shaky, and although she had toyed with the notion of clenching her fist and taking a swing at him, she refrained. She was too weak to do any damage, and he would surely kill her.

And now her mental faculties were eroding. Even under the influence of alcohol, she would never dream of the three or four main men in her life arguing over her, and even in her worst nightmares, neither Joe nor George would openly criticise her darling Colin like that.

What was her deteriorating mentality trying to tell her? That she would soon be joining Colin? Peace at last?

To her horror, she found the prospect had some appeal. If nothing else, her death would end this persistent terror.

A new resolve overtook her. She was not old, she was not in the grip of some terminal illness. She would survive, she would live on, and one day, when she was the lively, energetic Brenda Jump again, she would seek out this lunatic and teach him what real fear was about.

Almost on cue, she heard the clanking of the steel door and a moment later, her jailer, her tormentor entered.

As always he was masked, as always, the two knives, one a theatrical prop, the other the real thing, were displayed at his belt. He carried food in one free hand, and his familiar video camera in the other, and placed both on the single table.

'You know the rules, Jump,' he said as he freed her hands. 'Behave yourself and you live.'

The food was basic, insufficient, bread and cheese, but Brenda ate with gusto. She needed the minimal energy it would provide.

'You'll need the bucket,' he said, as he released her ankles. 'After that, you've a final video to make.

If your pal Murray does as he's told, it'll be over tomorrow. If he doesn't it might be all over for you, but a different kind of all over.'

Brenda felt suddenly emboldened. 'You're underestimating him.'

'I don't think so. He's always been a mouthpiece but he could never fight.'

It was an error. Like bringing the heater which allowed Brenda to see more of her surroundings, he had made a primary mistake. Could she get the message across to Joe or whoever was receiving the videos?

# Chapter Eleven

Both having received copies of the latest video the previous evening, Joe and Sheila met outside Gale Street police station at a few minutes after nine on Saturday morning.

'Did you notice how much she was blinking?' Sheila asked as she led the way in.

'I did,' Joe agreed, 'and I gave Les a call. He's promised to be here this morning.'

Even as Joe said it, Tanner appeared, striding at a brisk, military pace from the Galleries shopping mall. Perfectly attired in his regimental blazer and tie, his shoes gleaming with a mirror finish, he greeted them with a grim half smile.

'Good morning, Sheila, Joe. You've had another video message from this lunatic?'

He was merely repeating what Joe had already told him, and it was Sheila who responded. 'She's blinking and blinking and blinking, Les, and as of now, we're certain she's trying to get a message to us.'

Tanner cast a demeaning glance upon Joe. 'We've had our differences over the years, Joe, but as you're aware, I value the 3rd Age Club and its members, and I'm only too happy to render whatever assistance I can.' He gestured at the police station entrance. 'Shall we?'

Convincing himself that Tanner kept a stock of such grandiose announcements for use when the pertinent situation arose, Joe ushered Sheila through, and the two men followed her.

They were escorted to the briefing room, which had become the temporary headquarters of the current investigation. Cummins, Gemma, and Dockerty were all in attendance, and alongside them, was an army officer in full uniform.

'Morning,' Cummins greeted them. 'Allow me to introduce Lieutenant Colonel Harcourt of the Army Intelligence Corps. Colonel, permit me to introduce Mrs Sheila Riley, Joe Murray, and Leslie Tanner, three very close friends of the lady who has been abducted.'

Harcourt, a man in his mid-40s, shook hands with each of them in turn. Joe and Sheila consigned themselves to a brief greeting but Tanner was more gushing, and Joe felt he only just stopped short of saluting the man.

'A pleasure to meet you, sir. Captain Leslie Tanner, Sanford Regiment. Retired.'

'A pleasure to meet you too, Captain. You're the chap receiving the video messages?'

'No, sir. Mrs Jump, the missing lady, works with Sheila and Joe, and although Chief Superintendent Cummins described us as close friends, I don't think Brenda has anyone closer than these two good people.'

Harcourt frowned. 'So your role, is, precisely what?'

At this juncture, Cummins interrupted. 'As I explained, Colonel, we believe Mrs Jump is signalling to us by blinking her eyes, using Morse code. Mr Tanner was with us yesterday and successfully translated the message. Brenda appeared to be saying, "nuclear bunker", which is the reason we contacted your department.'

Harcourt resumed his seat, Joe, Sheila, Tanner, took their places around the table. The army man obviously had his doubts. 'No disrespect to the lady in question, but she probably would not know what a military nuclear bunker looks like. Indeed, with the possible exception of yourself, Superintendent, I doubt that any of you would.'

Cummins would not be beaten. 'When you see the videos, you'll realise why Mrs Jump might have come to that conclusion. For now, Joe, Sheila, you have fresh videos?'

They handed over the memory sticks. 'Have you spoken to Lofthouse?' Joe asked.

Passing the memory stick to Gemma, Cummins nodded. 'I have, and yes, he received one too. We're waiting for one of his people to deliver it.'

Joe noticed that aside from himself, Sheila, and Tanner, everyone was wearing forensic gloves. He could not understand why. None of the previous memory sticks had produced any trace of fingerprints other than his, Sheila's, and those of other people who had handled them, presumably the staff at the Gazette.

At length, Gemma had her laptop running and kickstarted the video.

As before, Brenda's face filled the screen. She was pale, looked ill, afraid, and there was the unmistakable sparkle of tears in the corners of both eyes. The sight served only to ignite Joe's anger. Notwithstanding his lack of prowess as a scrapper, if he could get his hands on this evil man…

Brenda began speaking, and as she did so, her eyes began to blink rapidly as they had in the previous video.

'I'm going to give... give you precise instructions for del... delivery of the... the ransom. It will be Joe Murray alone. If... if I see anyone else any... anywhere nearby, the ransom will not... not be collected, and Brenda... Brenda Jump's life will be end... ended.'

The electronically harsh voice of her captor broke in. 'Just read it. Never mind dithering.'

Brenda looked up presumably into the eyes of her tormentor. 'I'm scared, you idiot. Scared of you, what you might do.'

Watching the performance, Joe felt a fierce glow of admiration run through him. Brenda had not yet lost all her fight.

She went on. 'Joe will deliver the ransom, twenty-five thousand pounds in cash. He will deliver it to the graveyard at St Jude's at midnight on Saturday. He will leave the bag behind the grave of Fiona Watson. I'm sure the police will pinpoint the exact location of the grave. Murray will not wait around. Having delivered the bag, he will leave immediately, and drive away. If there is any deviation from these instructions, if there is anyone else in the vicinity, Brenda... Brenda Jump will be executed.'

A sob caught in Brenda's throat, and the video blacked out.

Joe broke the silence which followed. 'Fiona bloody Watson.' He glowered at his niece. 'This is Vic Atherton. It has to be.'

'Wrong,' Gemma insisted. 'Fiona bloody Watson, to echo your temper, wasn't buried as Fiona bloody Watson. She was buried as Fiona bloody Atherton. I told you the other day, didn't I? Vic married her shortly before she died.'

'Yeah, but—'

Dockerty cut him off. 'There's no gain in falling out between ourselves, Joe, Gemma.' He focused on Tanner. 'Can you tackle the blinky-blinking, Les?'

'Only too happy to take it on. Can I have that small room again and a copy of the video where I can focus on it?'

Gemma took one of the memory sticks, and escorted Tanner from the room. The moment they were gone, Joe rounded on the remainder.

'I don't care what Gemma says. This has to be something to do with Atherton. Haven't you tracked him down yet, Terry?'

'Obviously not, otherwise we'd have told you. Just clue me up on this, Joe. You exposed Atherton as a thief at the shop where he worked, and Fiona Watson worked there too, didn't she? What price another member of that crew could be working this scam? Gemma told you, this isn't Atherton's style, and like she said, if it was him, he'd refer to her as Fiona Atherton. But the people who worked at the Yorkshire Jewellers would know her as Watson, wouldn't they?'

Joe found it impossible to refute the logic. 'All right, you're right. Even so, I don't think we can discount Atherton. The only other two people I can recall involved in that business were the shop manager and the regional manager. Paul Webber was the manager. You must know him, Terry. He's a Sanford lad. His boss was, er, Alex somebody or other. Can't remember his name. Based in Leeds I think.'

'I'll get some people onto it, Terry,' Dockerty said and took out his phone.

'You'll find Paul in the local branch, Mr Dockerty,' Sheila said. 'It's in Galleries. I'm sure plenty of Terry's people know him.'

Dockerty raising eyebrows at Cummins nodded his permission, and the Leeds-based detective, got onto his phone.

While he was making the call, Joe focused on the military man. 'Well, Colonel, do you have anything to add?'

Harcourt toyed with his cap. 'Superintendent Cummins showed me some of the enhancements his people had done from the previous videos, and I have to say, it does look like a bunker of some description, but according to our research, there are no nuclear bunkers in the Sanford area. Perhaps Captain Tanner knows better.'

Joe delivered a derisive snort. 'Les was only ever a Territorial. He wasn't full time and he's been retired a good few years.'

'Irrelevant,' Harcourt said. 'The TAVR receives the same training as full-time, enlisted men and women. He may never have seen enemy action, but he will be well-trained to deal with it, and his knowledge of both the military and this local area will be much better than mine. As for nuclear bunkers, we have them all over the country. I suppose some of the best known are in Oxfordshire and they were designed for—'

Joe cut him off. 'Oxfordshire? We had this debate the other day, and it's a non-starter.'

'I don't know, Joe,' Sheila commented. 'Dorothy lives there, doesn't she?'

'Yes, but you spoke to her on Wednesday and she knows nothing. It doesn't make sense, anyway. If he's taken Brenda to Oxford, how's he gonna pick up his ransom at St Jude's? If he's commuting to and from there, he'll need most of the twenty-five grand for petrol.' He rounded on the colonel. 'Wherever he has her, it has to be in this area.'

Harcourt shrugged. 'In that case, you're better off relying upon Mr Tanner rather than me.'

Dockerty rejoined the discussion. 'Vinny Gillespie's on his way over to speak to this Paul Webber. He'll get the name of his regional boss from there, and I'll bell our people in Leeds – assuming that's where he lives – and get someone to speak to him. Joe, when you tackled this Atherton, how many others of the shop's staff were involved?'

'None. It was just Paul, the manager, the man who called me, his regional boss, this Alex somebody or other, Atherton, and Fiona Watson. Atherton and Watson were working together, and living together I think. Whatever, they worked together to nick this expensive ring. It was a clever setup, but they didn't fool me, and when I confronted them, with Paul and his boss standing by, Fiona Watson broke down and virtually admitted everything. I'm not saying it couldn't be one of the other members of the shop's staff, but I didn't have anything to do with any of them.'

It was left to Sheila to bring up a fresh angle. 'As I recall, Joe, you were there alone, and there for less than a day. Neither I nor Brenda had anything to do with that case.'

'Granted,' Joe conceded, 'but let's be honest about this, Sheila, we're known all over Sanford, me, you, and Brenda, so it's fairly certain that other members of staff at that shop would have known about us.'

'It could be broader than that, Joe,' Cummins said. 'Think about this. You've just said you're known all over Sanford, all three of you. I'm not arguing with that. Atherton's escape – for want of a better word – is also well known all over town. Hell, we've been looking for him for the last three or four days, and it's been all over the Gazette, and it's even made the radio and TV. All it needs is for someone in this town to tie it all together, bag Brenda, decide upon Fiona's grave, and that would lead you – and us – to think it's Atherton. You see what I'm getting at?'

'Yes, but it would still have to be someone who could tie Atherton to both me and Fiona Atherton, and they would have to know that Fiona's name was Watson.'

'We're going round in circles here,' Dockerty intervened. 'I suggest we wait and see what Vinny has to say when he's spoken to the shop manager.'

On a nudge from Sheila, Joe glanced at his watch, read 9:45, and said, 'Yes, well, we're only waiting to see what Les has to say, then we'll have to leave it to you. We have a café to run.'

'Yes, Well, before you leave we have another point to take up, don't we?' Cummins said. 'Tonight. St Jude's. Will you do it, Joe? We'll make sure you're well protected. We'll have a presence in the area.'

'No you bloody well won't. I'll do it, Terry, but I'm not risking Brenda's life on this. I'll do as this nutter is demanding.'

'We can't risk that, Joe,' Dockerty said. 'do that, and this idiot may take the cash, clear off and leave Brenda to rot. We have to organise some cover for you.'

Joe delivered a sly smile. 'Why don't you leave me to handle that end of things? Me and the 3rd Age Club.'

Cummins disagreed. 'I'm not leaving this to a gang of vigilantes.'

In order to divert their attention, Joe asked, 'Have you sorted the money out? I mean it takes some doing getting 25K together, doesn't it?'

'It's organised,' Dockerty told him, and then focussed on Cummins. 'Terry, what say we fit Joe up with some kind of tracker? We can stay well back and move only when we know what's what.'

'We already have a tracker in the bag,' Cummins admitted, 'but, yes, it might be to our advantage to have Joe fitted with one.'

'And where will you put it?' Joe asked. 'In my boxer shorts? Besides, why do I need it? All I'm gonna do is drop the bag off.'

'I'm responsible for your safety,' Cummins said, 'and we're not taking any chances with this lunatic.'

Joe might have argued further, but at that moment, a perplexed Tanner and Gemma returned.

'This could take a little working out,' Tanner said. 'I believe she is telling us something, but it doesn't make a great deal of sense.'

He laid a single sheet of paper on the table. It was covered with various interpretations, until he had spelled out his final analysis.

HE GNOWS POE CNAT FIKHT

One by one, the people around the table picked it up and read it.

'I don't think it's that difficult,' Sheila said. 'Gnows? That obviously should read "knows". Cnat? Let me ask you, Les, how close of the two letters A and N in Morse code?'

Tanner consulted his personal printout of the code. 'Very close. A is dot-dash. N is dash-dot. You're indicating that Brenda got them the wrong way round?'

'Obviously,' Sheila said. 'If we translate it that way, the message reads, "he knows poe can't…" I believe the final word is fight. Again, Les, are G and K similar in Morse?'

'Not too far apart,' Tanner admitted after checking his crib sheet again. 'G is dash-dash-dot, and K is dash-dot-dash. On that basis, I would agree with you, Sheila.'

'So the only word we have to translate is poe, and looking at the spelling, and considering the overall message, I would suggest it should read Joe.'

For the third time, Tanner consulted his

printout. 'You know, I do believe you're right, Sheila. P is represented by dot-dash-dash-dot, and J is dot-dash-dash-dash. Given Brenda's obvious fear and her lack of in-depth knowledge of Morse, it's perfectly acceptable.'

Sheila wallowed in her triumph. 'In that case, gentlemen, and, er, lady, the message reads, "he knows Joe can't fight".' She smiled upon her boss. 'A reference to your legendary inability to get into a scrap, Joe.'

Joe was not in the slightest bit offended. 'And as far as I'm concerned, that narrows it down even further. Whoever he is, he's from Sanford.' He rounded on Cummins. 'I reckon it's time you got your boys out and about looking for Vic Atherton.'

Alongside him, Harcourt appeared a little bemused. 'I have to say, I feel like a fifth wheel here. Surplus to requirements.'

'Not so, Colonel,' Cummins assured him. 'If Brenda is held in some kind of military bunker, we'll need your expertise on the best way of getting into it.' He turned to Joe. 'You've a business to run, so you can get yourself back there but first we need to make arrangements for tonight.'

# Chapter Twelve

Joe agreed to return to the police station at ten that night in order to be fitted with a tracking device. Sheila insisted that she would be with him, even though he made it clear that she would not be allowed to accompany him to the churchyard.

'We can't risk it, Sheila. I have to be alone when I get there.'

She remained half-adamant. 'In that case, I shall ensure I'm here at the police station until you return. Assuming Mr Dockerty and Mr Cummins have no problem with that.'

The police yielded to her insistence, and on that note, Joe, Sheila, and Les Tanner left the station, made their way to the multi-storey parking area of Galleries Mall, where they bid farewell to Tanner and climbed into their cars for the two-mile drive to The Lazy Luncheonette.

As he drove along, Joe accessed the hands-free option on his mobile, and rang George Robson. 'I need a favour tonight, George. Any danger you can stay sober to give me a hand?'

'Come on, Joe. It's Saturday.'

'It's also for Brenda.'

George tutted. 'Go on, then. What's the score?'

'Not over the phone. Make your way to The Lazy Luncheonette and bring Owen with you. There's a free breakfast in it for the pair of you.'

'We'll be there in half an hour. Oh, while I think on. You wanted to know about Debbie

Atherton. Give Alec Staines a ring. As I remember right, he did her place up a couple of years back, so he'll know where she lives.'

Joe grinned to himself. 'Thanks, George. I'll see you at the café.'

Running away from Sanford town centre, Doncaster Road was one of the town's busiest thoroughfares, but a mile out of town, it became a free-moving dual carriageway, and Joe could focus on his plans.

It had occurred to him the moment the kidnapper's instructions were delivered. Yes, he would be alone when he delivered the money, and yes, he would leave immediately, climb into his car and drive away. Anything to ensure Brenda's safety. But would he go home? Not likely. And if this evil man was watching for police vehicles, would he be watching for ordinary, everyday cars, like George Robson's or Owen Frickley's? Never in a millennium plus one.

St Jude's was on York Road, a single carriageway which passed through largely residential areas, before drifting out into the open country on its way north. With George parked in a side street in the residential part, one with a view of St Jude's lychgate, and Owen tucked into a layby in the more rural area, both would spot any vehicles passing in either direction. It might make the perpetrator of this awful crime wary, and it might make him pause for a while, but given the age of the men's cars, so old that the police would never use them, it wouldn't raise any undue alarm.

At least, that's what Joe hoped.

And when this madman collected his ransom, they would be there; Joe, George, and Owen, and if necessary they would beat Brenda's location out of him.

It was a curious counterpoint to Joe's usual attitude to violence. He did not approve. Fighting, he had long ago learned, solved nothing. That mindset was influenced by his non-existent fighting skills. As a child, he learned that he could not beat even the weakest opponents in a fist fight, and in the schoolyard he relied upon people like George, Owen, Alec Staines, even Sheila and Brenda, to protect him. His fighting ability never improved with age, and despite his irritability and outspokenness, he would go out of his way to avoid such confrontations.

This head-to-head would be the exception that proved the rule. This man's treatment of Brenda was inexcusable, and if it needed a good beating to force him into revealing her location, then so be it.

He pulled in and parked at the rear of the café alongside Sheila, and disconnecting his phone from the hands-free set up, he rang Alec Staines as he climbed out of the car.

'Hey up, Joe. What's to do, mate? News on Brenda?'

'Not so you'd notice, Alec. I spoke to George a while back, and he suggested I ring you. Debbie Atherton. You know her?'

'Yeah, I know her. Did her exterior paintwork a couple of years back. Big fancy place on Calder Terrace. That's off York Road, just before you get to St Jude's. What you asking about her for? Has she been bagged too?'

Alec's announcement only firmed up Joe's suspicions, but he elected not to go into the matter. Instead, he said, 'No, nowt like that. It's her ex-husband I'm more interested in, Vic Atherton. I need to speak to her about him. What number Calder Terrace?'

'I'll have to look it up, Joe. Offhand, I think it's number one, but I can't be certain. I'll text it to you. Gimme five, ten minutes.'

'Good on you.'

As he made his way in through the rear door, his phone clamoured to announce an incoming call.

'Popular this morning,' he grumbled as he checked the menu window and read "Gemma". He made the connection. 'Gemma. Haven't you seen enough of me for one day?'

'Probably. We drew a blank at Yorkshire Jewellers, but we've had a thought, Joe. When you were up in Inverness, you twigged some killer up there, and he tried to run for it, but Brenda stopped him. Remember? It just dawned on us. You and Brenda, and our current blagger is targeting you and Brenda.'

'I can see what you're getting at, but I'm buggered if I can remember his name. Tell you what, get onto the big cheese at TeleP—' he pronounced it "telepee". 'Fella named Otis someone or other. He'll tell you who you're talking about. But whatever his name, he'll be walled up in Scotland somewhere. He's a million miles from Sanford.'

'No stone unturned, Joe. Yeah?'

'Let me know.'

After the breakfast crowd were gone, the café was never especially busy on a Saturday, and discounting the clutch of reporters and photographers pacing the pavement out front – smaller than it had been – this Saturday was no exception.

That was good for Joe. It fitted with his early plans, as he explained to Sheila and Cheryl. 'I don't care what the cops are saying about Vic Atherton, I need to speak to his missus. I'm expecting George Robson and Owen Frickley any time now, and when I've dealt with them, if you guys can hold the fort, I'll get over and hassle her.'

'You're still convinced it's him?' Sheila demanded.

'No. That's not what I'm saying, but after Brenda's latest message, it has to be someone who knows me. Atherton knows me, he has a grudge against me, he's AWOL from the nick. Plod haven't found any trace of him, and according to Gemma, his missus – correction – ex-missus hates him. She might just be able to give me a lead on him.'

Cheryl sneered. 'Great. So you send him back to the slammer. What about Brenda?'

'Calm down, girl. If he's got Brenda, then we'll have him, and if it isn't him, don't worry about it. Me and George and Owen will have summat sorted out before I'm due at the cemetery tonight.'

Now both women groaned.

'You and George Robson and Owen Frickley?' Cheryl exclaimed. 'Between the three of you, you couldn't organise a drunk's night out in a brewery.'

'Amen,' Sheila commented.

Joe tapped the side of his nose. 'George and Owen are getting a free breakfast out of it, so you just wait and see. If we don't have this bloke nailed and Brenda home by tonight, my name's not Arlington T Cuttlefish.'

His attempt at humour brought frowns from the two women.

'The police said they'd provide a discreet presence,' Sheila remonstrated, 'and you pooh-poohed the idea. You weren't willing to risk Brenda's life.'

'Sheila, the cops will be there. I'm not daft. I know Terry Cummins and Ray Dockerty, and they won't take a blind bit of notice of me. They'll be well-hidden. But if they nick this loon he won't talk. He can't afford to. Difference is, me and George and Owen can make him talk.'

'Beat the crap out of him, you mean,' Cheryl protested.

Joe gave her a throwaway shrug. 'If that's what it takes.'

'It's just one of George's less savoury habits,' Sheila said through tight lips. 'I have serious concerns about this, Joe. If it goes wrong, you could really be risking Brenda's life.'

'And her life's not already at risk? Listen to me, Sheila, if the filth get this guy, all he has to do is keep his mouth shut. They can't rough him up to make him talk. He can sit tight and leave Brenda to starve to death. We can force it out of him. For God's sake, we've all seen *Dirty Harry*. They would never have found that girl if Clint Eastwood hadn't forced him to tell him where she was.'

'Yes, and when they found her she was already dead,' Cheryl reminded him.

'And you don't have a gun and you're not going to face him across a football field,' Sheila observed.

Joe would not hear their complaints. His phone beeped to indicate an incoming text message, and as he made ready to open it, he said, 'Trust me. I know what I'm doing.'

Sheila had the last word. 'That will be a first,' she said as she walked away.

Barely had she returned to the counter when George and Owen walked in and ordered breakfast from her.

'I spoke to Joe, and it's a freebie,' George said.

Sheila's lip curled. 'So I've been told.' She wrote the order out, passed through the hatch to the kitchen, and poured tea for the two men. Pushing the beakers across the counter, she nodded in Joe's direction. 'Dirty Murray is waiting for you over there.'

Owen frowned. 'Dirty Murray?'

'He thinks he's Clint Eastwood. I'm sure he'll tell you all about it.'

When they joined Joe, he was studying the text message.

'What's this about you being Clint Eastwood?' Owen asked.

'Ignore it. Alec Staines has just texted me Debbie Atherton's address, so when we're done here, I'll be going to see her.'

George chuckled. 'You've no chance, Joe.

Why would she look at you when she knows I'm still available?'

'Tell me something, George. Does your thinking ever come above waist level?'

'It depends how big a top set she's got. In Debbie's case—'

'Just shut up,' Joe interrupted. 'We can make some kind of arrangement for tonight. I'm delivering the ransom in the graveyard at St Jude's at midnight. Atherton is sure to be watching, so I can't have anyone with me.'

'Just a minute, Joe,' Owen cut in. 'You're saying it's this Atherton guy?'

'I don't know for sure. I'm just assuming it's him. Anyway, like I was saying, whoever he is, he's going to be watching, so I can't have anyone with me. What I need are you two guys, parked close, but not too close to St Jude's. One of you in a side street on the Sanford side, the other somewhere on York Road in case he goes that way. I'll drive away after I've left the money behind, but I won't be going back to Gale Street or home, or anywhere. I'll turn round, say, half a mile from St Jude's, and wait until I hear from either of you. If we can keep in touch on the phones, the minute you see anyone come out of the graveyard, turn up in a car, or whatever, you bell me, and we get after him.'

'And what good will that be to Brenda?' George demanded. 'He's not gonna lead us to her, is he?'

'Yeah well, that's when the Clint Eastwood business kicks in. What we do is, we nab him, us three, and we make him tell us where she is.'

As Cheryl arrived with their meals, Owen frowned. 'All right, tough guy, how are you gonna persuade him?'

'I'm not. You are. You two.'

George understood at once, and as Cheryl set his meal before him, he smacked his right fist into his left palm. 'Now I understand. Just leave him to me, Joe. I don't care how tough he thinks he is, he hasn't met my knuckles.'

'Good on you, George. I don't approve of your scrapping, but in this instance, I think it's the way forward.' Joe got to his feet. 'Enjoy your meal, both of you. Right now, I'm going out looking for him… via his ex-wife.'

# Chapter Thirteen

If Alec Staines are done much to reinforce Joe's suspicions, the siting of number one Calder Terrace served only to confirm them. The street ran off York Road to the left, and because the Athertons' place was the first house on the left of that street, it had a clear view of St Jude's a hundred yards further up York Road. It would allow Atherton to monitor Joe's movements when he delivered the ransom twelve hours hence. That, in turn, would mean he could also watch for any movement immediately after the drop was made, and it would allow him any length of time before moving to collect his blood money.

Not that it would necessarily alter Joe's overall plan. Atherton might have the patience of Job, but so did Joe, and he was certain that George and Owen would be willing to sit it out. Anything that would help rescue Brenda from this evil man's clutches.

As Staines promised, it was a large, three or four-bedroomed house, with a small, front garden, and broad bay windows at ground level, expansive, three-light windows on the first floor, and as if that was not enough, there was a dormer window jutting out from the roof. Ample viewpoints for Vic Atherton to keep his eye on the church.

Joe parked, climbed out of the car, pulled his topcoat around himself to shut out the February wind, and ambled to the front door, where he rang the bell. While he waited, he looked over the front lawn, sad and shabby in its winter shroud. A small tree – Joe hadn't a clue what kind – stood to one corner away from the door, its branches bear, barren, no sign of pre-spring budding.

Getting no answer, he rang the bell again, and through the frosted glass of the door, he could see a shape moving towards him. A moment later, the door opened, and Debbie Atherton scowled down at him.

'Yes?' The tone was sharp, bitten, laced with acid.

Determined to demonstrate his own irascibility, Joe responded, 'How do you know? I haven't asked you anything yet.'

The reply puzzled her. 'Who are you, and what you want?'

'I'm Joe Murray. I run The Lazy Luncheonette, Doncaster Road.'

'I've never heard of you.'

'Well you should have done. I'm the one who sent your old man to prison after he and his girlfriend nicked that ring from Yorkshire Jewellers.'

'Oh, that was you, what it? So what do you want?'

'A word, if it's convenient. Preferably inside, out of the cold.'

She stood back, let him in, and she closed the door and led the way along the hall to the kitchen, where she turned and announced, 'If you're looking for Vic, you're looking in the wrong place. I've had the police round, and I told them, I haven't seen him. And if I did see him, I'd hand him back to them.'

Joe walked to the table, pulled out a chair without waiting for an invitation and sat down. With what he believed was an engaging smile, he looked her up and down.

In her mid-50s, about his height, she had been a good-looking woman once over, but time, and no doubt, the stress of divorce had taken its toll. Her blonde hair was pulled back into a tight, short ponytail, her ice blue eyes treated him to a chill matched only by the inclement weather outside. She was a little heavier than George's enthusiasm had led him to expect, and her voice, which he had no doubt could turn on the seduction, was just as bitter and angry as that same weather.

'I don't apologise for nicking your husband. I'm a private detective, when I'm not serving bolshie truckers, and I do as the people who pay me ask.' It was not entirely true. At the time of the Yorkshire Jewellers' request, he had never charged for his services. With an eye on her wedding, engagement, and eternity rings, he went on, 'What I don't understand is why Vic would leave a good-looking woman like you for that little tramp he was working with, that Fiona Watson.'

Once again, it bore little resemblance to the truth. As he recalled, Fiona Watson was a good deal more attractive than the woman stood before him now. If, however, he hoped his flattery would thaw some of Debbie Atherton's chill, he was mistaken.

'Cut the smarm and get to the point.'

'Have you ever thought of joining the Sanford

3rd Age Club? I'm the chairman, you know, and we're a sociable bunch.'

'I've asked you once to cut it out and get to the point. What the hell do you want?'

Joe gave up the unequal task. 'All right. I'll be honest with you. Just in case you haven't heard, or you've been on the moon for this last week, one of my friends, Brenda Jump, has been kidnapped. Your old man is in the frame.'

She shrugged. 'Yes? And?'

'I can't go into too many details, but I notice you have a cracking view of St Jude's. Funnily enough, that's where Fiona Watson – or Atherton as she became – is buried. I had an idea you might be hiding Vic here.'

She laughed. A harsh, staccato cackle, flooded with derision. 'I've seen it on the news, and I've read the reports in the papers. They talk about you and this woman's other friend, Ripley, or someone.'

'Riley,' Joe corrected her.

'Well, all I can say is if that poor woman is relying on someone as puddled as you to help, she's dead meat.' The hint of humour faded and disappeared as quickly as it had come. 'Get this straight, Mr private detective, I haven't seen that pig since you sent him down, and if I do see him again, the police won't have much to send back to the nick. Do you understand?'

'Perfectly.' Joe got to his feet. 'But there's something you should know, Mrs Atherton. Puddled I might be, but don't let that fool you. I don't go away, and I can't be scared off. If I find even one trace of your old man linked to you, I'll be back, and next time, I won't be on my own.' He fastened his coat. 'I won't apologise for disturbing you, because like you, I prefer honesty to porkies. I'll bid you good day.'

He took no more than two or three steps towards the kitchen door before she stopped him. 'Just a minute.'

He turned, raised his eyebrows at her.

'Do you seriously imagine that Vic could be involved in something like kidnap?'

'A lot of the fingers point that way. It's not definite, but whoever's doing this is using Brenda to have a go at me, and your ex is one with a beef against me.'

'You're giving him a level of intelligence he doesn't have. Let me tell you something, Murray, he couldn't plan his way from here to York, and it's a straight road. Look at the way he made a mess of that robbery at Yorkshire Jewellers. Him and that little tart, Watson, had a perfect plan, but it didn't pan out like that, did it? They made a complete hash of it, and they were lucky that the management didn't spot it earlier. We were already separated at that time, and we were waiting for the divorce to be finalised, but he was too gormless even to get on with that. He's a simpleton. There is no way that he could plan kidnap, hide the woman away somewhere, and then produce these videos which the police are allegedly receiving from the Sanford Gazette. I'm not saying he's totally thick, but he is. Look at the way he got caught nicking that car. The one he got sent back to prison for. Got into a ruck with the owner in a pub, owner dropped his keys,

Vic picked them up, went out, stole the car, and spent three days riding round in it. Anyone with an ounce of brains would have sold it. But not Vic. He's a dork, a total berk, and okay, so they reckon that his time inside has toughened him up a bit but this kind of advanced thinking, planning, is beyond him. If you're looking for someone who's bagged your girlfriend, don't waste your time looking for Vic.'

Joe nodded. 'Thanks. And this time I mean it. I'll bear it all in mind. I'll see myself out, Mrs Atherton.'

A minute later, he stepped out into the bitter afternoon, climbed into his car, started the engine, took a couple of shunts to turn the car round, and drove back out onto York Road, but he did not turn right towards the town centre. Instead, he turned left, cruised along the road, then swung over to the right, to park outside St Jude's, where he sat with the engine running.

If Debbie Atherton thought she had laid his suspicions to rest, she was wrong. Straining his memory, he calculated that she and Vic Atherton had been divorced for between two and three years, and yet she was still wearing a full set of wedding, engagement, and eternity rings. He would admit that he wasn't exactly an expert in such matters, but in his narrow experience, most divorced women removed such jewellery, and if she had hit it off with George Robson, she surely would not have worn those rings when she met the 3rd Age Club's gadabout, supposed playboy.

After a few minutes, he killed the engine,

climbed out, locked the car, and once again wrapping his overcoat around himself, he walked through the lychgate, into the churchyard where he veered off to the right into the cemetery.

St Jude's was an old church. It had stood there since the early days of the Sanford colliery and the foundry, and he had the idea that the cemetery was no longer in use. Full, or very nearly. His parents were both buried in the graveyard at Sanford Parish Church, so he wasn't one hundred percent certain, but St Jude's was a busy cemetery, and he knew it would take him some time to find the grave of Fiona Watson.

He wandered along the paths between ranks of graves, seeking the newer headstones. According to Gemma, and indeed Kayleigh, Fiona had been buried about a year ago, so surely she would not have been dropped into a communal grave.

As he walked along, looking left, looking right, he cast occasional glances back at Calder Terrace, and no matter where he was in the graveyard, he could still see the Athertons' home. His earlier deduction had been correct. That place was perfect for observing activity in this sad burial ground.

He found the grave eventually, marked with a simple cross in black marble, bearing her name and age. He was surprised to learn that she was only 44 years of age when she passed away. The information sent a shaft of sadness through him, and brought out memories of Denise Latham, his lady friend, who was just a few years older when her life ended. Denise, of course, was murdered, Fiona passed away through a vicious, unrelenting illness, but no matter which way he looked at it, that age was no time for anyone to come to the end of their life.

From this position, he had a clear view of Calder Terrace, and once more, it served to reinforce his suspicions. More than that, it persuaded him that Debbie Atherton was not simply hiding her husband, she was involved, if only at the planning stage.

Making no effort to hide himself, he cast his memory back to the incident in Yorkshire Jewellers a few years earlier, focusing on an image of Fiona Watson as she was then.

An attractive, shapely, freckle-faced redhead who was clearly attached to Vic Atherton. Were that not the case, had Joe met her in a bar, he would have been attracted to her. And what of her now? A collection of bones interred in a wooden box, nothing to say she had ever existed aside from this black cross bearing her name, and her memory used, abused by a pair of criminals.

The chill began to seep through his overcoat and he made a steady way back to the car, climbed behind the wheel, ran the engine to warm up the heaters, and asked himself what would Debbie Atherton stand to gain from involving herself in this evil scheme, if only in the planning. A throwaway comment from George Robson came back to him. How she, Debbie, was always complaining about the cost of living and a lack of money.

Parked on the wrong side of the road, he turned the car round against the oncoming traffic, and drove back towards Sanford. The police would not listen to him. He knew that. But he also knew that he was right, and come midnight he would demonstrate the accuracy of his deductions.

# Chapter Fourteen

By the time Joe got back to The Lazy Luncheonette, the crew were in the process of cleaning down, ready for the traditional Saturday early closing.

Leaving the work to Lee, Cheryl and Kayleigh, he drew Sheila off to one side and told her of the things he had learned on his expedition to the Athertons' home. She listened patiently and when he was through, took a moment to formulate her thoughts.

'So she chooses to wear her wedding and engagement rings. It means nothing, Joe. She could be wearing them as a reminder of her disenchantment with her ex-husband. Or perhaps she has some good memories of her marriage, and wants to preserve them.'

'And if that's the case, what price she's hiding Vic in one of the upper rooms and she's just given me a load of flannel?'

'I'm not saying you're wrong. I'm simply saying it may not be as significant as you imagine.' She sipped on a cup of tea. 'Of more significance, I think, is the view from her house as you've described it. Given night glasses, she – or even Vic – would be able to keep an eye on you wouldn't they?'

'My thoughts precisely, but they'll come unstuck. I won't do anything other than drop the ransom and then drive away. It'll be up to George and Owen to do the rest.'

'Or more likely, the police.'

With a sad smile, the kind usually reserved for the naïve and innocent, Joe said, 'I know you have a lot of faith in the cops, what with Peter being an inspector and all, but this time, Sheila, I believe the only way we'll get Brenda back alive is to deal with it our way.'

'We shall see. For now, what's the procedure tonight?'

'I have to be at Gale Street for ten to be fitted with this tracking oojah. I'll leave there about eleven-thirty to make sure I'm in time at St Jude's. After that, it's whatever happens.'

'Yes, well, as I said this morning, I'll be at Gale Street with you and I'll stay there until we know it's all over. Don't look at me like that,' she remonstrated when he pulled an ugly face. 'Brenda is our friend. I'm as concerned for her as you are. Do you seriously think I could sit at home and do nothing but worry? She's going to need a lot of support and when, if they find her, I want to be there.'

Joe capitulated. 'Fine. Whatever you say. For now, you'd better get off home and try to snatch some sleep. It's gonna be a long night.' He drank his tea and got to his feet. 'Lee, Cheryl, Kayleigh, it's time to call it a day.'

'Yeah, but we've still some cleaning to do, Uncle Joe,' Lee protested. 'The floors to mop and stuff.'

'Leave it and get off home, all of you. I'll deal with it.'

Kayleigh hurried to him. 'You will let us know

how you get on with looking for Brenda, won't you, Uncle Joe?'

'Count on it,' he promised. 'Now get your coat and bugger off home. All four of you.'

They did not argue further. Instead they removed their whites and tabards and a few minutes later, Joe was left alone in the café, pottering with the unfinished cleaning Lee had worried about. Washing up the few remaining dishes and cups, his thoughts were focussed on the coming night.

The prospect worried him. He was not afraid, merely concerned. If things went wrong, if his plan to track down the kidnapper went awry, it would not be him, George, Owen, Sheila, Tanner, or the police paying the price, but Brenda. A practical man, one who lived by the code that problems were there to be confronted not evaded, he nevertheless found the thought of losing one of his best friends unpalatable. He found himself recalling the times he had spent with the woman, not all of them in a bed. She was a party animal, a woman who had suffered the worst kind of pain when she lost her husband, but who recovered with an attitude of life's too short not to enjoy yourself firmly entrenched in her being. The world, the country, Yorkshire, Sanford, the 3rd Age Club, Sheila Riley, and Joe Murray did not deserve to be without such a gregarious woman.

And as he finished the menial jobs, he vowed that it would not happen. One way or another, he and his friends would win and Brenda would come back to them.

He left via the rear door and drove home, taking his time, refusing to be rushed by other road users.

He had six hours to kill before he was due at the police station, eight hours before dropping off the ransom, and the only outstanding task, as far as he was concerned, was a quick word with George and Owen, telling them to keep away from Calder Terrace. It was too much to hope that the pair would get through any evening, let alone a Saturday without taking in a few beers, and he had no doubt that they would be in the Miners Arms early on. He would catch them there before going to Gale Street.

Lacking the drive, the willingness to cook, he chewed his way through a frozen Lancashire hotpot, then hit the sofa intent upon grabbing an hour's sleep before getting ready for the coming night.

Pointless. No matter how hard he tried to close his mind, Brenda still occupied his thoughts and feelings, and her plight only generated more anger in him.

TV was no distraction, and at eight o'clock, he gave up all pretence at distancing himself from the forthcoming trial (which was what he considered the prospect to be) took a shower, shaved, and dressed appropriately in a pair of black, jogger jeans, a dark jumper and black trainers. With the time coming up to nine, he put on his dark, quilted topcoat, left the house and drove to the Miners Arms where he found George and Owen in the lounge bar.

After securing a glass of lemonade, he joined them.

'Delivering chocolates instead of the ransom, Joe?' George quipped.

Owen laughed, Joe didn't, and Owen felt

obliged to explain. 'You look like the Milk Tray man. And what are you doing drinking lemonade?'

'I need to stay stone cold sober, so shut it, the pair of you.' Joe took a moment to calm down. 'Now listen to me. I don't know which way you've got it worked out, but whoever's parking closest to St Jude's, keep out of Calder Terrace.'

George groaned. 'Not Debbie and Vic Atherton again? I told you, Joe, it's nothing to do with them.'

'And you might be right, which would be a first, but after seeing her this afternoon I have more information than you, and they're still in the frame, only this time, it's the pair of them.' George was about to interrupt, ask what information, but Joe pressed on before he could speak. 'Remember, both of you, we're doing this for Brenda, and we don't want to give the game away, so keep clear of Calder Terrace. Right?'

'Whatever you say, buddy,' Owen agreed. 'George is handling that end of things. I'll be on York Road. There are a couple of side streets about five hundred yards up past the church and I'll be in one of them.'

Joe took a healthy swallow of his soft drink. 'Good. Phones on all the time. George, you're the main man. My end of things should take less than five minutes. I know where the grave is, so it's only a case of nipping in there, dropping the bag, and coming out. The scrote will be watching. When you see me come out, get into my car, turn round and drive off, watch for him, her, or it making his move. He'll have to be mobile, so he'll turn up by car. I'll be further down York Road back towards town. The minute you see anything, bell both of us, tell us what kind of car to look out for and which way it's headed. You got all that?'

'I've got it, I've got it. I'm not thick, you know.'

'No. Just boozed up most of the time.'

Owen brought up the logical objection. 'Suppose he's on foot? And suppose he goes over the far wall of the church?'

'Then we're snookered,' Joe admitted. 'Bear in mind, no matter what Terry Cummins and Ray Dockerty told me, the filth will be there somewhere, and if he goes that way, they'll have him. He'll know that, so he's more likely to be mobile, and if so, we can't afford to bugger this up, and for Brenda's sake, I'd prefer us to get him before the cops.' He drank off the lemonade and half rose, preparing to leave.

Owen stayed him 'One thing, Joe.'

He sat down again, 'What?'

'Suppose you go into the churchyard, and he's waiting for you, and he batters you. And you don't come out again?'

Dismay etched into Joe's cragged features. 'Thanks, Owen. You're doing my confidence the power of good.'

'He has a point, though, Joe,' George said. 'What we do? Bell the filth?'

Joe shook his head. 'Ring Sheila. She'll be at the police station and she can get the message to Terry a lot quicker than you going through the switchboard. Ten to one, the cops'll have someone nearby, if not actually in the churchyard, but no matter what, if I don't come out after a few minutes, you and Owen get into St Jude's and see if you can grab him. Yes, and while you're at it, give him a good kicking from me.' His head wandered from side to side, looking at both men. 'Anything else before I shoot off to Gale Street?' When neither man brought up anything, he went on, 'In that case, I'm on my way. You two need to be on station by no later than, let's say, half past eleven.' He got to his feet again. 'I'm on my way. Let's hope it all comes together, huh. I'll see you guys later.'

His nerves were jangling when he climbed into his car and set off for the police station. Owen's last point had never occurred to him until it was pointed out. He would be outside the church for a few minutes to midnight, but for all he knew, the kidnapper could well be there already. It was not a pleasant prospect.

Cummins, Dockerty, Gemma, Sheila, and Les Tanner were all waiting for him when he was escorted into the briefing room. Harcourt was there too, although for the life of him, Joe could not imagine what the military man might be able to add to their efforts.

The atmosphere was grim, concerned, and when Joe joined them, Cummins went straight into his briefing.

'Now that we're all here, I'll run through our plans again. This is for your benefit, Joe. I don't care what this scrote has demanded, we'll have people in the area. We'll have a tracker on you, and the ransom already has a tracker installed in the bag. I'm not stupid. I know you'll have people out and about, as well. No heroics, Joe. And don't look at me like that. I mean it. You take the ransom, go into the graveyard, leave it there, and come out again. You get back into your car and drive away. There's a remote chance that this clown will be waiting for you. If so, just do as he tells you. I repeat, no heroics, no stupidity. If we register that your tracker is static for longer than a minute or two, we'll send our people in. You understand all this?'

Joe nodded. 'And where are you going to fit the tracker?'

Cummins looked down at Joe's footwear and tutted. 'What the hell are you wearing? Take your shoes off. We have a pair of police issue boots ready for you. What are you? Size eight, nine?'

Sheila chuckled. 'He takes a six.'

'Bugger,' Cummins cursed. 'Too late to worry about it. We have a pair of size eights for you. We'll have to jam some wadding in the toes.'

'Wrong, Terry. How am I supposed to walk in shoes that are two sizes too big for me?'

'I don't care how you walk, Joe. You can plod along like a circus clown for all I care. These boots have been fitted with a tracker set into the heel, and we've already tested it. It's up and running. So stop moaning and get them on.' He looked to Gemma. 'Can you get them for him, please?'

She nodded, and left the room.

'I have a couple of queries,' Joe announced. 'First, if you get this guy, how will you make him talk? You know the script, Terry, Ray. All any lag has to do when you pull him in is keep his mouth shut. The right to silence, remember?'

'Just leave that to us, Joe,' Dockerty said. 'We have ways of persuading them, and I don't mean beating the crap out of him.'

Cummins confirmed it. 'Right now he's looking at abduction, demanding money with menaces, ill-treatment of his victim. If he doesn't tell us where she is, he's looking at a potential murder charge, or at the very least, attempted murder. He'll get a lot longer for that than he will for kidnapping.'

'Yes, well, you'll excuse me if I don't share your confidence. Another point. How do you know when he leaves the church, he'll go to Brenda?'

'We don't. That's why we have officers in the area.' As Gemma returned with the boots, Cummins pointed a warning finger at Joe. 'I told you. No heroics. Don't try to negotiate with him. If you're faced with him, just do as he says. We'll handle everything from there.'

Gemma handed him the boots, and Joe's dismay registered further. 'This is bloody stupid. I don't think I could even drive in these. I'll change into them when I get to the church.'

'No you won't,' Cummins ordered. 'You'll put them on now and leave your trainers with us.' He hurried on to forestall Joe's complaints. 'We're not taking any chances, Joe. If this idiot is close by, checks out your car and spots a spare pair of shoes, it'll be a red light to him.'

Joe was beaten into submission, and with a degree of grumbling, removed his trainers, handed them to Sheila, and put the boots on. Sheila handled the trainers gingerly, and Gemma supplied her with a bag to put them in.

With the boots in place, Joe stood, and paced around the room, his feet clodhopping on the laminate floor, bringing smiles to everyone but him.

'I'm walking like a model from a stop-start animation.'

'You'd certainly never pass muster on a parade, Murray,' Tanner said.

'Be careful, Les, or I might put this boot toe where you wouldn't like it.'

Over the next hour, silence was largely the order of the night, and at 11:30, Joe, carrying the ransom – wedges of fives, tens and twenties – in a plain paper bag, walked out of the police station, climbed into his car, and with a small audience comprised of the men and women from the briefing room watching, drove off for his rendezvous.

It was a little after a quarter to midnight when he stopped by the lychgate of St Jude's. He had already decided to wait ten minutes before leaving the car to carry out his mission.

He was not a happy man. The boots were uncomfortable, the outside chance of coming face-to-face with the kidnapper preyed upon his mind, and he had to force himself to think of Brenda in order to bolster his nerve.

With hindsight, had he considered the prospect, he would have switched the engine off, but he left it running to stave off the cold of the night. With a few minutes to go before he left the car, the driver's door yanked open, a hooded figure crouched low so as to keep out of sight, and with his gloved hands, pressed a knife against his neck.

The familiar, electronically altered voice, spoke to him. 'Into the passenger seat, Murray. Try anything stupid, and you're dead.'

# Chapter Fifteen

Afraid for his safety, his very life, Joe did not argue. He moved into the passenger seat, and the kidnapper took the driver's seat and slammed the door shut.

'Face the passenger window, hands behind your back. Do it. Now.'

Once again, Joe obeyed, half turning, slipping his hands behind his back, pressing his face to the window and staring across at Humber Grove, where George's battered Peugeot stood on the corner. He prayed that his friend was actually looking this way.

He felt thin rope wrapping round his wrists, and an unpleasant memory came to him. Two murderous criminals hell bent on burning him and Denise Latham to death, tying him to a chair, but as they did so, he tensed his muscles. He knew that once the rope was tied and he relaxed it would loosen the binding. He did it again now resisting, tensing every muscle in both arms, hoping that in the darkness, the kidnapper would not realise.

And then the job was done. Joe relaxed, and tested the strength of the bindings. As he guessed, he had the slightest play in them.

'Face front,' came the order, and Joe obeyed.

His abductor slotted the car into gear, checked the mirrors, and drove off, along York Road, away from Sanford. Joe anticipated his phone ringing at any moment, but his tormentor was ahead of him. As they drove along, he reached into Joe's pockets, found the phone, and switched it off.

'It's just you and me, Murray. We don't want any hangers on, do we? Especially that clown parked on Humber Grove.'

So he knew about George. Would he also know about Owen? If so, he said nothing when they shot past Owen's Ford parked in a side street a quarter of a mile from St Jude's.

Forcing his voice to remain steady, angry, Joe asked, 'You really think you're gonna get away with this?'

'I'm not doing too bad to press, am I?'

A half mile further on, as they ran into open country, the kidnapper pulled the car into a layby, and Joe watched while he opened the paper bag, removed the blocks of money, jammed them into a Sainsbury's carrier bag, then let down the window and threw the police bag out.

'You and the cops really think I'm stupid?' He laughed as they drove off. 'That thing probably has a tracker taped into the linings. They'll find it wherever the wind blows it.'

And for the first time, Joe was grateful for the oversized police boots and the hidden tracker in the heel.

\* \* \*

At Gale Street, confusion reigned. As the clock hands approached midnight, Sheila's phone rang, followed a moment or two later by several telephones.

Sheila listened to George Robson's urgent call,

her face a mask of shock and alarm, Dockerty listened to the officers stationed in the vicinity of St Jude's, and he was an angry mass of concern. While that was happening, Cummins and Gemma listened to the report from the tracking station.

'He didn't deliver the money,' Dockerty said.

'George says he just drove off,' Sheila declared.

Cummins called for quiet. 'The trackers have the bag stationary about a mile along York Road but Joe is still on the move.'

Sat towards the rear of the room, Harcourt contributed for the first time that evening. 'It looks as if your friend Murray was the kidnapper all along, and he decided to disappear with the ransom.'

His announcement was met with a howl of protest, the most vociferous coming from Les Tanner. 'With respect, Colonel, I've known Murray for half a century, and although we don't always see eye to eye, I can assure you, that man is as honest as the day is long.'

Sheila supported him. 'Along with me, Brenda is one of his closest friends, and there is no way that he would put her through this kind of torture for the sake of money he doesn't need.'

'All right, all right, let's all calm down,' Cummins insisted. 'Sheila, what did Robson have to say to you?'

All attention focused upon her. 'Rightly or wrongly, Joe stationed George Robson in Huber Grove, a side street close to St Jude's, where he could keep an eye on events. Owen Frickley was parked further along York Road in another side street. According to George, Joe arrived at about quarter to midnight, and five or six minutes later, he saw the driver's door open, and he was expecting Joe to get out. But it didn't happen. Instead, the door closed, and a minute or two later, Joe just drove off.'

'Wrong,' Gemma said. 'Joe wouldn't do that. You know that as well as I, Sheila. It's more likely that the kidnapper was lying in wait, and when Joe stopped, he sneaked in and took over the car. God knows what he might have done to Joe.'

Cummins agreed. 'You're right, Gemma. We all know Joe, and for Brenda's sake, he wouldn't duck out of what he had to do tonight. We must assume that the kidnapper has Joe.'

Tears sparkled in Sheila's eyes. 'Joe alive... or dead?'

Cummins remained grim. 'We have no way of knowing, so let's remain optimistic. And if nothing else, we still have the tracker in Joe's boots.'

A stern silence fell over the room. Tanner broke it several minutes later. 'Remain optimistic, you say, Terry. Could it be that he's taking Joe to leave him with Brenda? After which, he'll simply disappear with the ransom.'

It was Dockerty who replied. 'Entirely possible, Mr Tanner. But if they're heading out of Sanford on York Road, where the hell are they going?' He gestured at Harcourt. 'The colonel has already said there are no nuclear bunkers in this area. Let me ask, where is the nearest in that direction?'

Harcourt was about to answer when Sheila

interrupted. 'Les, the Sanford Regiment. Weren't you based out that way?'

'Yes, we were, but that base was closed a long time ago. And anyway we didn't have a nuclear bunker there, because obviously, this area was never considered a first strike target. We had nothing like a—'

Harcourt cut him off. 'You had a training bunker, Captain. Am I right?'

A look of horrible realisation spread across Tanner's tired features. 'Oh my God. You're right. And as far as I know, it's still there.'

'With electricity?' Sheila demanded.

'Chances are the MoD never got around to cancelling it, especially if the land is up for sale,' Harcourt said.

Cummins whirled on him. 'How do you get in through those steel doors?'

Before the colonel could respond, Tanner spoke up once more. 'The steel door is inside the building and it doesn't lock. The actual access was nothing more than a wooden door. The key was issued to whoever was in charge of training when the place was used, but it's so old and clapped out, that I imagine anyone could get in with a crowbar, and as I said the internal steel door was never locked. Too big a risk of idiot recruits locking themselves in or out.' The urgency in his eyes begged them to understand. 'Consider the situation. Brenda has been tied to that chair all week. Why? She's a prisoner. Why keep her bound hand and foot?' He did not wait for an answer. 'Because if she were free to move around, she would have learned that the place was not locked. She could have walked out at any time.'

Cummins snatched up the phone and barked orders into it. 'All teams out to the old Sanford Regiment base. Get an ambulance on standby. No sirens, no emergency lights, get a bloody move on.' He slammed the receiver down. 'Ray, Gemma, let's get out there.'

Sheila stood and Tanner ranged himself alongside her. 'Brenda will need some serious support.'

'And Murray too, more than likely,' Tanner said. 'We're coming with you, Superintendent.'

'Les, Sheila, I appreciate your concern, but I've just ordered an ambu—'

Sheila interrupted, 'We're coming with you, Terry, so deal with it.'

\* \* \*

The old Sanford Regiment base was a decrepit mess, long overdue for demolition.

That thought ran through Joe's mind as his captor turned into the base.

It had not been used for years and Sanford Borough Council could not afford to level the place. That aside, he had an idea that the land was the property of the MoD and it would be up to Whitehall to find a buyer willing to take it on, clear the site and then build houses, industrial units or whatever on it.

It was also the logical place to bring Brenda and now him.

He had never paid serious attention to Les Tanner's tales of military glory. As a part-timer with the Territorials, the man had never travelled any further than somewhere in the Wiesbaden area of Germany, and the most serious enemy action he'd seen was his occasional 3rd Age Club contretemps with Joe and other long-serving members. Be that as it may, he recalled Tanner detailing their training sessions, one of which was "in the event of nuclear conflict breaking out".

It was so obvious that Joe silently cursed himself for not having thought of it sooner. Sanford had no bunkers of any description, but the old training base had a mock-up of one and before his captor pulled up outside the small blockhouse, Joe knew it was where Brenda had been held for the week.

As the car engine died, the knife came to his throat again. 'I'll be coming round your side to let you out. Try anything stupid, and I'll slice you. Understand?'

Throughout the fifteen minutes since leaving St Jude's, he had wriggled at the bindings and they had begun to slacken, but not enough for him to take any stupid risks, and the candour, the outspokenness for which he was known forbade Joe answering other than with a nod.

The passenger door opened, and the kidnapper dragged him out. Memory bells rang through Joe's mind. Yorkshire Jewellers, the wanted poster. This person was a similar height to him and therefore could not be Vic Atherton who was described as 5'11". Well wrapped up, hooded and masked, there was nothing which could be used as identification, but there was one thing Joe could test.

As he came out of the car, he stumbled and fell into the attacker, who pushed him back. 'Careful or it'll be your last move.' The knife flashed in the night and Joe shrugged an apology.

Again, he was careful not to speak. He needed his hands free, he needed to see Brenda before he could open his mouth, but the deliberate move had confirmed his theory. He knew who the kidnapper was, he knew why it had all happened. All he had to do now was shut up until the right moment, if such a moment showed up.

He was pushed through the flimsy, ramshackle wooden door on the outside of the bunker, and confronted with its steel counterpart ahead. His fury rose when the kidnapper just opened it. No key. It was not even locked. If she were not tied to that chair, Brenda would have walked out whenever she pleased.

And talking of Brenda, she was slumped on the chair, eyes closed, head lolling to one side. He had no idea whether she was sleeping, unconscious or… Joe buried the thought before it could properly mature.

Without waiting for instructions, he rushed to her, turned his back and crouched slightly so he could nudge her with his bound hands. She stirred, moaned and as he turned to look upon her, her eyes opened and a faint smile crossed her pale lips.

'Joe.' Her voice was not much above a whisper, barely audible. 'I knew you'd come. Is Colin with you?'

Delirium. A week of terror, a week bound to that chair, a week without proper food or rest, had scrambled her thought processes. This woman whose intellect was never less that acute, whose humour was one of the mainstays of his friendship with her, reduced to a rambling shell.

His fury enveloped him and this time he did not hold back. He rounded on the kidnapper. 'What have you done to her, you crazy bitch? And why? Because you're broke after your old man went down and you couldn't milk him for a decent divorce settlement? If that's how you are, I don't blame him for jumping Fiona Watson.'

It was a pivotal moment. In the act of hurrying towards him, Debbie Atherton stopped, yanked off her hooded mask, ripped away the vocoder, and glared at him. 'You knew. That's why you came to my place this afternoon.'

'Wrong. I came to your place to find your ex. It was only when I went to the churchyard that I realised you could be working together.'

Joe took two paces forward, his police boots cracking on the stone floor. He stopped when her knife appeared.

'I was gonna bell the filth, tell 'em where to find you,' she hissed, 'but I've changed my mind. I'm gonna slice you now, let you bleed to death and leave that bag to starve while I disappear with the money.'

She came at him. Joe looked frantically around, seeking a means of warding off her attack, but there was nothing, and even if there was, how would he get hold of it? Why did he imagine that he could get out of the bindings? As he recalled, it didn't work too well the last time he tried it.

Looking death in the face, no way to defend himself, he took a step back and his boots rapped the floor again.

The boots! Hadn't he insisted he didn't want them. Why? Because he hadn't expected anything like this.

She rushed towards him, and at the last moment, he kicked out. The toe of his right boot rattled her shin. She yowled. Joe kicked again, this time at the other shin. She dropped the knife, and then went down, scrabbling for it. Joe moved, brought his boot down on her outstretched wrist and she screamed.

'You broke my wrist.'

Kicking the knife beyond her reach, he growled, 'Be thankful I only hit your wrist and not your empty head.'

She began to slide across the floor making for the knife. Joe positioned himself in front of her, blocking the way and all she could see was his boot toe.

'Take a look it, crazy lady. The cops fitted a tracker in it. If I know anything about Terry Cummins and Ray Dockerty, they'll be here in the next few minutes, and you're on your way to a comfy little cell for a good few years.'

\* \* \*

It was a good ten minutes before the police, led by two armed officers, burst in. When they shouted the all clear, Cummins, Dockerty, and Gemma entered followed by Sheila, Tanner, and a brace of paramedics.

Joe greeted them with a crooked smile. 'Where you've been?'

Cummins scowled, Dockerty laughed and said, 'We had to deal with a lock-in at the Miners Arms first, Joe. We settled for a coupla pints.'

While Constable Noel Wickes unfastened the bindings at Joe's wrist, and the paramedics began their work on Brenda, Joe gave both senior officers a run down on what had happened at St Jude's and since.

'You have questions to answer,' Cummins insisted. 'I warned you about vigilante action, didn't I?'

'What vigilante action, Terry?' Joe waved at Debbie Atherton. 'I might have broken her wrist when I trod on it, but that was self-defence. If I hadn't stopped her, she'd have knifed me and left Brenda to starve. As for George and Owen, well they were just keeping an eye on things in case your people failed.'

'And they did a good job,' Sheila said. 'George rang me right away when he saw your car drive off, Joe.'

With her wrist strapped up, uniformed officers either side of her, Debbie glowered. 'How did you know it was me?'

Joe smiled back. 'Your booby-doos. When I bumped into you as we got out of the car, your chest gave way. If you'd been a man that wouldn't have happened.'

'You…' she moved towards him, but was restrained by the police.

They led her away, and Joe told Cummins, 'Check out her place, Terry. I'm not saying you'll find Vic Atherton there, but you never know.'

'We will, and we'll want a statement off you.'

'Not tonight, Superintendent,' one of the paramedics said. 'He needs to come with us for a full health check.'

'I'm all right,' Joe insisted.

'So you're a doctor as well as a wannabe Clint Eastwood?' Sheila argued. 'Go with them, Joe. I'll be along soon after you.'

'Yeah, but my car…'

'I'll ring Lee and he'll come out to get it home for you. Now go with the paramedics and stop arguing.'

# Chapter Sixteen

A grey dawn showed through the distant windows when Joe, insisting he was fine, discharged himself, and emerged from the A&E treatment area to join Sheila and Gemma in the waiting area.

Both women greeted him with a hug and after paying due courtesy to their attention, he sat with them. 'Brenda?'

Sheila shook her head. 'We're still waiting. Let's be honest, Joe, she's in a bad way.'

'She's tough. She'll recover.' He focused on Gemma. 'The Atherton woman?'

His niece let out a long yawn. 'Paramedics taped up her wrist – you did crack the bones, by the way – and she's on ice at Gale Street. We'll need a duty solicitor, and as far as I'm aware, Ray Dockerty is ready for tackling her. Don't worry about it, Joe. We've got her banged to rights, and by the time we're done, she'll be joining her old man for a long stretch.'

Sheila frowned. 'What was it all about? I mean why did she do it?'

'Money,' Joe told her. 'She was strapped for cash after Vic went down for nicking that ring.'

Gemma pursed her lips. 'I don't see what that has to do with you and Brenda.'

'We're well known, all of us, and I think she saw Brenda as an easier target than me.'

Following his niece's example, Joe, too, yawned, and went into a detailed explanation as he had told Cummins several hours earlier. Both women were appalled when he spelled it all out.

'All that ever mattered to her was money,' Joe concluded. 'George told me as much, said she did nothing but moan about the cost of living and stuff. I reckon that in her eyes, when I nailed Vic, she was the one losing out.' Again he concentrated on Gemma. 'And talking of Vic, did you get him?'

'Not as far as I know, but there's an outside chance that she'll know where he is. It wasn't his voice on the videos, obviously. Analysis hasn't officially come through yet, but it was her. We're sure of it. Don't worry about Vic Atherton, Joe. We'll get him. I can tell you that he wasn't at her place, but I've already been informed that the search team did find several rings and a gold watch, inscribed "to Brenda, with all my love, Colin". They figure Debbie took them from Brenda when she first abducted her. If you're right about her money problems, she probably planned to hawk them off.'

'Colin bought the watch for her fortieth birthday, as I recall,' Sheila said.

'A good man, Colin Jump,' Gemma concurred. 'And you two should be thinking about her not the Athertons.' She glanced at her watch. 'Quarter past seven. I wish they'd hurry up with her.'

'What are you doing here anyway?' Joe asked.

'I volunteered, didn't I? I've known you three for most of my life, and Terry Cummins needed someone to wait here on the off chance that we might get a statement from Brenda. Because I know you so well, I put my hand up.' She let out a sigh. 'I don't hold out much hope. That's if they ever let us see her.'

'She was very weak when I got to her,' Joe said. 'Rambling, too. Chances are they'll keep her in for a day or two, just make sure she's all right.' He took Sheila's hand. 'Remember when that dipstick tried to poison you? You moved in with Brenda for a week, didn't you?'

She smiled. 'I'm ahead of you, Joe. Once we've seen her, I'll make my way home, and get the spare bedroom ready. Then I'll call at Brenda's, pick up some clothing for her, and she can stay with me.'

Joe said nothing. It was exactly as he had expected.

Another half hour passed before a young doctor, her eyes heavy with the need for sleep, approached them. 'You're waiting for news of Mrs Jump?'

'We are,' Joe agreed.

'She's awake but very weak. She's in shock, suffering from dehydration, mild exposure, and possible dietary issues. We'll need to keep her for at least forty-eight hours. Beyond that, she's going to need someone to care for her at least for the next few days.' She frowned. 'Are you her partner, Mr Murray?'

Joe could not help but laugh. 'Not bloody likely. Brenda and I discussed that once before. We're great friends, but if we lived together, it would be World War Three in a matter of days.' He nodded to Sheila. 'Mrs Riley will take care of her when she's discharged.'

'Good. That's all we need to know.'

'Can we see her?' Sheila asked.

'We're about to move her to a ward, but yes, you can have a few minutes with her. If you'd like to follow me.'

Gemma spoke up. 'Excuse me, Doctor. DI Craddock, Sanford CID. What are the chances of getting a full statement from Mrs Jump?'

'Slim. Non-existent, to be honest. First, we don't want to take any chances by compelling her to remember the trauma she's been through. Second, she's still in shock and she tends to slight delirium. Any statement you took, probably wouldn't make much sense.'

Gemma nodded her agreement. 'In that case, I'll leave you, Joe, Sheila. I'll ring the chief, and then get myself home to bed. Give Brenda all my love, and I'll see you both later.'

'You take care, Gemma,' Sheila said.

'Call in at The Lazy Luncheonette for a free bite when you know something,' Joe told her.

As Gemma left, they followed the doctor through to the treatment area, and into a curtained off cubicle, where Brenda appeared to be asleep.

She looked pale, haggard, drawn, and the moment he laid eyes on her, Joe's anger rose. 'I should have jumped on that cow's head while she was laid out.'

Sheila hastened to calm him. 'The police have her, let them deal with it. Like Gemma said, our concern is Brenda.'

She must have heard their voices. Her eyes flickered open, darted between them, the tears welled and she began to cry. Sheila hurried to the bedside, took a chair, reached across and wrapped her arms around their distressed friend. Joe stood by feeling guilty. Women who cried always made him feel guilty, even when he had nothing to be guilty about.

At length Brenda calmed down, broke away from Sheila's arms, and held out hers for Joe. He came to her, and she pulled him down, hugged him as tightly as she could, but he noticed that there was a little strength in her arms.

'I don't know how I will ever repay you.' As if confirming her general debilitation, her voice was frail, distant.

Joe kissed her on the cheek. 'Not just me, Brenda. I was the fall guy. The bloody idiot appointed to come and meet that crazy bitch. There are plenty of other people who've been fighting for you, not least, Sheila.'

He broke away, pulled up a second chair, and sat alongside Sheila. Brenda turned to that side, and held both of them by the hand.

'Les Tanner translated your efforts at Morse code,' Sheila explained. 'He and I were at the police station late last night while Joe was out delivering the ransom, and when we traced him, Les came along with me to show us the way to that bunker.'

'And we had George and Owen standing by, ready to tail the woman if necessary,' Joe said. 'Alec Staines dug out the Athertons' address for me, and I was suspicious of her the moment I met her.'

'In fact, Brenda, the whole of the 3rd Age Club

was pulling out the stops on your behalf.'

'And the Sanford Brewery draymen, and Lee, Cheryl, and Kayleigh at the café.'

'It goes further than that. I believe most of Sanford had their eyes open for sign or sight of you.'

Brenda began to cry again, and silence ensued until she had calmed once more.

Eventually, when her emotions were under control, she said, 'They're going to keep me in, the doctor said. Just for a couple of days, make sure I'm all right.'

'And after that, you'll stay with me for a week or two,' Sheila told her.

'I don't want to put on you—'

Sheila cut her off. 'Like I didn't want to put on you after that nonsense the other Christmas? No arguments, Brenda. You're going to need looking after for a while.'

'And don't worry about your wages,' Joe assured her. 'I'll make sure you're paid everything you're due.'

There was another stilted silence before Joe chimed up once more. 'After that business with Sheila and that nutter, we all shot off to Tenerife to help her recover. We're thinking about taking you to Benidorm. When you're well enough to fly.'

Brenda sniffed back her tears. 'That's a damn good idea, Joe. A 3rd Age Club trip?'

'That's the plan. I'll put it to the members at the next meeting. But you are gonna have a slight problem, Brenda. You'll be paying for our beer all week. In recognition of our efforts this week.'

'No, Joe. You're the one who'll have the problem once I have my strength back. Because every single night that we're in Benidorm, I'll be thanking you in my own special way for saving me.' Brenda gave them a weak smile, and it generated a round of pleasant laughter.

Still smiling, Joe shook his head, leaned over and kissed her once more. 'Some people never change, do they?'

**THE END**

THANK YOU FOR READING. I HOPE YOU HAVE ENJOYED THIS BOOK. WOULD YOU BE KIND ENOUGH TO LEAVE A RATING OR REVIEW ON AMAZON?

# The Author

David W Robinson retired from the rat race after the other rats objected to his participation, and he now lives with his long-suffering wife in sight of the Pennine Moors outside Manchester.

Best known as the creator of the light-hearted and ever-popular **Sanford 3rd Age Club Mysteries**, **Mrs Capper's Casebooks** and in a similar vein the Spookies Paranormal Mysteries. He also produces darker, more psychological crime thrillers as in the **Feyer & Drake** thrillers and occasional standalone titles sometimes under the pen name **Robert Devine**

He, produces his own videos, and can frequently be heard grumbling against the world on Facebook at https://www.facebook.com/dwrobinsonauthor where you're more than welcome to **follow me and my work**.

He has a YouTube channel at https://www.youtube.com/user/Dwrob96/videos. For more information you can track him down at www.dwrob.com and if you want to sign up to my newsletter and pick up a **#FREE book or two**, you can find all the details at https://dwrob.com/readers-club/

# All books by David W Robinson

**The Sanford 3rd Age Club Mysteries**
The Filey Connection
The I-spy Murders
A Halloween Homicide
A Murder for Christmas
Murder at the Murder Mystery Weekend
My Deadly Valentine
The Chocolate Egg Murders
The Summer Wedding Murder
Costa del Murder
Christmas Crackers
Death in Distribution
A Theatrical Murder
Killing in the Family
Trial by Fire
Peril in Palmanova
The Squire's Lodge Murders
Murder on the Treasure Hunt
A Cornish Killing
Merry Murders Everyone
A Tangle in Tenerife
Tis the Season to be Murdered
Confusion in Cleethorpes
Murder on the Movie Set:
A Deadly Twixmas
Naked Murder
Murder at the Christmas Meddlercon
Missing With Menaces
**Special Editions**
Tales from the Lazy Luncheonette Casebook
Boxed Set #1

**Mrs Capper's Casebooks**
Mrs Capper's Christmas
Death at the Wool Fair
Blackmail at the Ballot Box:
Exit Page Ten:
A Professional Dilemma
Murder at Christmas Manor
A Call to Murder
Death of Innocence
Death at the Diet Club
The Christmas Festival Murder
A Quizzical Drowning
Scarborough Not Fair
A Cryptic Christmas Cat-Nabbing
Series Page

**The Midthorpe Mysteries**
A case of Missing on Midthorpe
A case of Bloodshed in Benidorm

**SPOOKIES Paranormal Mysteries**
The Haunting of Melmerby Manor
The Man in Black

**Feyer & Drake**
(Published by Bloodhound Books)
The Anagramist
The Frame

**Thrillers written as Robert Devine**
Dominus
The Power
Kracht
The Cutter (Published by Bloodhound Books)

## LOOKING FOR A COUPLE OF FREEBIES?

Then why not sign up to my newsletter. I guarantee you will not be spammed and I'm not in the business of selling email address. You'll receive not more than two or three emails per month, but best of all when you sign up to, you'll be guided to a page where you can download not one but TWO FREE BOOKS.

Visit https://dwrob.com/readers-club/ for details.

Do you want to know where I'm up at any given time? Then why not follow me on Facebook?

You have the following options. Follow me on my Facebook author page or you can join reader groups at David W Robinson & Readers and Ex DSK Crime Writers or you can do all three.

I welcome comments and feedback on both Amazon and Facebook.

Go on. You know you want to.

Printed in Great Britain
by Amazon